INSPIRED BY MINDY

A SWEET ROMANTIC COMEDY

REMI CARRINGTON

PHREY PRESS

A great new job, a gorgeous new place to live, and the most frustrating landlord in the world. I guess I can't have everything I want.

The Cowboy Chef has a reputation as a heartbreaker, but that doesn't stop my heart from going pitter-patter whenever he's around. It's not because I'm over forty and single. There are other reasons.

But I'm not going to risk opening my heart to man with his reputation. Any man for that matter.

Then I end up living across the driveway from him, and he calls a truce. Being nice to each other only makes my heart-thumping worse.

He oozes charm like the sun gives off heat. But it's clear he's not interested.

When we're stranded in a freak snowstorm, I snap and unleash a heap of brutal honesty.

His response catches me completely off guard. What do I do now?

❦ Created with Vellum

CHAPTER 1

MINDY

*E*verything needed to be perfect.

Tapping my clipboard, I walked to the entrance of the venue. Getting the same view as the attendees would help me see if anything needed to be changed. Even though my new boss was out of town, word would get back to her, and I wanted her to hear how well the event had gone and that I was an asset.

After accepting the job, I'd done my research and found nothing but good things written about the people who owned the place and worked here, except for one person. The guy who often catered events—people called him the Cowboy Chef—had a reputation. I'd have to watch out for him, but based on the rants I'd read, I was a little old for him. Not that he was young. He just dated young'uns.

Running my finger down the page, I walked as I scanned my checklist, making sure it all looked amazing and seeing what still needed to be done. Every box had a check mark in it.

The welcome sign near the entrance matched the name on the paperwork, but the grass was just tall enough that it brushed the bottom. The sign would stand out better if weeds weren't growing in front of it. I yanked on one of the offending plants, but it didn't want to come out of the ground.

I ran back to my office, rummaged through my desk, and grabbed the scissors. There was more than one way to take care of a problem.

On my hands and knees, I snipped the grass or weeds or whatever they were, cropping them close to the ground. Now, nothing blocked the sign.

As I stood and dusted off my knees, I shook my head. Trimming grass with scissors was a bit excessive, but attention to detail and overthinking were my specialties.

Once the scissors were safely back in my drawer, I continued my walkthrough. I looked into the gathering rooms and strolled past the food table. The caterer hadn't yet arrived, but Ava had said he was on his way.

The Christmas lights were draped in trees and along the fences, and they twinkled. That tree on the far right bugged me. Whoever had done the lights had bunched the strands together in one place. It detracted from the full effect of the holiday lights.

I hurried back into the building where the offices were. "Ava, do we have a ladder around here?"

"If I tell you where to find the ladder, you must keep the location a secret." Ava pointed at me, reminding me of my second-grade teacher who'd liked to use chalk as her pointer of choice.

"Do you have a problem with ladders being stolen in these parts?" I made sure Ava understood the humor in my question. The venue wasn't close to much. The nearest town wasn't very big, and there were more cows than people within a two-mile radius. Theft probably wasn't much of an issue here.

She shook her head. "Not theft. *Men*. Beau fell off and broke his leg. Clint nearly stranded himself on top of a barn, and . . ." Her smile widened. "Mad Dog used it to come after me. They are convinced that it's their *lucky* ladder. I keep it hidden so no one else gets hurt, and I finally found a new hiding spot." She peeked out the door like we were on a spy mission, then motioned for me to follow her.

We walked around the back of a building, Ava looking over her shoulder multiple times as we went. Then she opened a barely noticeable door. "There you go. Just put it back when you're finished. And if anyone ever needs it, get it for them. Don't tell them where it is."

"All right." Biting back a grin, I carried the ladder to the tree and climbed up. A lucky ladder. That was funny.

Adjusting the lights shouldn't take too long, but I had to be careful because I wasn't dressed for this type of work. Not that it had stopped me from kneeling in the grass.

I inched out onto the branch, trying not to snag my slacks.

The strands were wrapped tight, and repositioning them took work. I shifted each strand bit by bit, adjusting the distance between them. What should've been quick work took longer than I anticipated.

A truck door slammed, and I peeked through the branches. The tall, well-built man striding this direction had to be the caterer. When I'd researched, several pictures of him had popped up. None of them had done him justice.

From my hidden vantage point, I stared. He didn't look like he was in his mid-fifties. His dark hair had very little gray, and there were noticeable muscles on his arms. The jeans and boots were a nice addition.

His deep olive complexion added to his good looks, and it was easy to see why women fell all over themselves around him. But I would not be one to join the ranks of those who giggled and fawned to win his attention.

He strode to the base of my tree, and I held my breath, not ready to talk to him. When we did meet, I wanted it to be face-to-face and professional.

Then that heartbreaker chef carried away my ladder.

Who would walk off with a ladder and leave someone stranded? Ugh. He leaned it against a post on the arbor covering the food table, lifted a string of lights out of a box, and started climbing, not caring that he'd left me trapped.

After a huff, I shouted at him. "Hey! Bring that back."

His head swung around, and his brow furrowed. Haltingly, he backed down the ladder. "Hello?"

"Put the ladder back. What part of that is hard to understand?"

His lips quirked into a smirk, and he strode toward the tree, but he'd left behind the one thing I wanted.

Readjusting, I slipped and then wrapped my arms around the branch, getting poked by little lights. "Are you trying to land me in the hospital?"

He looked up at me, and that smirk transformed into a full grin. "Need help getting down? I can catch you." He held out his arms and danced his eyebrows.

The nerve of this man.

"No, I don't want you to *catch* me. I want you to put the ladder back." I didn't even attempt to maintain a polite tone.

"What are you doing up there?"

"Spacing the strands of lights." I sighed. "Will you please get the ladder?"

"Sorry, yeah. I didn't see you in the tree." He carried it over and leaned it against the trunk. "You can come down now. I'll hold it while you do."

"Just back away. I got up here without anyone holding it. I should be fine getting down without help."

He was the one person whose help I especially didn't need. I didn't want to encourage him in any way.

I climbed down without problems until the third rung from the bottom. He was too far away to be blamed for shaking the ladder, but something shifted, and as my foot slipped, I braced for a hard collision with the ground.

Arms wrapped around my waist, and a very firm chest pressed to my back. He set me on the ground but didn't let go. "Hello. I'm Jeffrey."

I whipped around and pushed away from him. If I stayed in his arms any longer, my knees would melt, and I'd agree to anything. "I know who you are." Reminding myself of all that I'd read about him, I pictured him with a short, curvy twenty-something on his arm.

His eyebrows lifted in surprise.

Ava waved as she hurried toward us. "Oh good, I caught you both together. Jeffrey, this is Mindy. She's the new event coordinator. You'll be working with her most of the time from now on."

"Fabulous." He smiled, but there was a hint of something else in his eyes.

Ava looked at me. "This is Jeffrey, the Cowboy Chef. He does a lot of the catering out here."

I made a show of looking him over. Normally, I was much more polite, but I needed this man to stay far away from me. "Your reputation precedes you."

His lips pinched, and he stuffed his hands into his pockets. "Ouch."

Clearly, he knew what I meant. As long as we had a good understanding, working together wouldn't be a problem.

CHAPTER 2

I flipped over a card and laid it on the table, enjoying a rare poker night. These didn't happen often, at least not with these guys. Because of Mad Dog, I was now included in the poker night gatherings and had gained friends. It was a nice change from life before. Hanging out with people my age had its advantages.

Occasionally, I sat in on a game with the ranch hands, but being around those guys made me feel old.

Mad Dog shifted cards around in his hand. "Did you meet the event coordinator?"

All eyes at the table focused on me. The other three were married, and there was no question who Mad Dog meant even though he hadn't looked up from his cards.

"You know I did." And I'd been thinking about Mindy since, but I wasn't going to share that tidbit with anyone.

Clint grinned. "And?"

"She told me that my reputation preceded me." I had no qualms sharing that with these guys. They knew enough about the old me to know what she'd meant, but they also knew how I behaved now.

Clint shook his head. "Ouch."

"That's what I said." I laughed, trying to cover the sting of her comment. Changing my behavior hadn't made people forget my previous actions. Nor did it erase things from the internet.

Mindy had formed her opinion from what others had said before she'd even met me. It bothered me, but I should've been used to it by now.

"Maybe she'll change her mind once she gets to know you. It worked for me with Lilith." Beau tossed a chip into the pile in the center.

"Nice thought, but Mindy seems a bit young for me." I appreciated having friends who motivated me to be better. Seeing the love they'd found kept me hopeful I hadn't forever missed the opportunity to share my life. I had at least a few decades left.

"You definitely shouldn't ask her how old she is." Clint slid a stack of chips to the center. "Raising twenty."

I groaned and laid my cards faced down on the table. "Fold. And thanks for the great advice."

The door to the game room swung open, and Ava carried in a tray. "Nachos are ready. I'll leave these right here." She kissed Mad Dog on the cheek, then grinned. "Oh, my! That's quite a hand." After another quick kiss, she patted his shoulder. "I'm headed home. Call if you need anything."

Mad Dog had an amazing poker face for someone who'd been a pastor. "Love you."

"Love you too." Laughing, she slipped out of the room.

Beau sighed. "She does that just to annoy me, and I hate it because I don't know if she's being serious or sarcastic." He looked at Clint. "What do you think?"

"I think I'm not going to give you any information because I prefer to win. It's getting close to Christmas, and I want to surprise Joji. Y'all are going to help me do that."

I grabbed a plate of food and sat back from the table. "By losing big all night?"

He pointed at me. "Bingo."

Beau tilted his head as he looked at his cards. "You buying her more goats?"

"Or another llama?" Mad Dog stared at Beau. "Any day now would be good."

He added two chips to the pot.

Clint raised again. "I'm buying us tickets to Paris, but I'm doing it on my dime. I want her to show me that little café."

The guys stared, stunned by the answer.

I wasn't. Clint would do anything for Joji. I'd nearly found that out the hard way when I tried to ask her out. My one attempt at dating someone closer to my own age hadn't gone well at all. No regrets. They loved each other, and everyone in the state probably knew that by now.

"Guys, I'm going to take off. Thanks for inviting me." I fished keys out of my pocket.

After everyone said their goodbyes, Mad Dog stood and extended his hand for a shake. "Ava said not to give up."

That comment answered a question I'd been noodling all day. Had Ava heard Mindy's comment? Ava had started to walk away and hadn't given any reaction, so I wasn't sure. Now I knew she had.

Reminding myself they were trying to be encouraging and helpful, I smiled. "Thanks."

My exchange with Mindy stung for multiple reasons. Not only had she judged me based on my prior actions, but I'd slipped so naturally into flirting with her even before getting a glimpse of her face. And that only confirmed to her that I hadn't changed at all.

But I had changed, and it had taken self-discipline and dedication. Even though those big blue eyes captivated me, I intended to stick to the promise I'd made to myself.

My integrity meant more than a pretty face and a nice evening.

But it would be easier to keep my promise without that pretty face in my thoughts every other second.

Working with her would be a problem.

CHAPTER 3

MINDY

This was supposed to be my golden hour, my opportunity to show my new boss what a great fit I was for the new job. But instead, I was cursing at brake lights. My Monday was off to a horrible start. It was the worst possible day for there to be an accident on the interstate.

Lilith, my boss, had gotten home from her delayed honeymoon trip, and the event I'd helped with when she was away had gone smoothly. But I'd only helped with those. Today's event was the first one I was running.

I slammed my steering wheel, avoiding the horn because that would only irritate already frustrated people. I had to let Lilith know I'd be late.

Resigned to the embarrassment and possible fallout of telling my boss I wouldn't make it to the venue on time, I called her.

After two rings, Lilith's chipper greeting echoed through my car speakers. "Hello, Mindy. Everything okay?"

I swallowed, determined to keep the emotion out of my voice. Showing weakness was not going to endear me to my boss. To anyone. "I'm so sorry. It's taken me over an hour to inch along the last five miles. There must be an accident on the highway."

"But you're okay?" As she asked the question, a bull wandered along the median and stopped to eat grass not far from my car. Thanks goodness I'd chosen blue. I felt bad for all the people in red cars.

Now I knew why traffic was snarled, but I wasn't any less irritated. Hollering at the bull would only get my car bashed, so I didn't roll down the window and give the beast a piece of my mind.

"Mindy?" Lilith sounded genuinely concerned.

"Sorry. I'm fine. Just very irritated." I'm not sure she'd believe me if I told her what was happening.

Two deputies wove through the stopped cars and positioned themselves behind the bull. With their cowboy hats in hand, they tried to coax the bull forward.

They weren't having much luck. It was probably easier to get a toddler to give up candy than to get a bull to go where he's not interested in going.

When a deputy looked toward cars behind me, I turned around to see if someone else was going to join in the excitement. A guy, who looked like he knew a thing or two about cattle, strode past my car—close enough I could read the label on the back of his jeans—and chatted with the deputy.

After some nodding and talking on the radio, the deputies and the cowboy managed to get the bull up the median a bit. Far enough that I could no longer see them.

This was crazy. At least at the venue, there were no cattle. All the bulls and cows were on the other side of a fence far away from my office. And that was good.

"I'm not sure how long I'll be stuck here." I didn't dare roll down my window, but I really wanted to see what was happening with the bull.

"I'll manage things here until you arrive. It'll be fine. Hang on." Mumbles sounded in the background before Lilith was back on the line. "Jeffrey is covering everything regarding the food, so that's taken care of. Be safe and get here when you can. And don't worry about it. Things happen."

"Thanks, Lilith."

Jeffrey was the last person I wanted informed about my tardiness. He was a chef with a fancy restaurant, and the definition of tall, dark, and handsome probably had his photo beside it. Even in his fifties, the man looked good. But discovering he had a reputation for dating much younger women and breaking hearts had helped me set boundaries from the very beginning.

Unlike the string of women who'd posted about him online, I wouldn't succumb to his good looks and charm.

He had both in spades.

When we'd met a couple of weeks ago at my first event, I'd somehow ended up in Jeffrey's arms. It felt way too good, and I wouldn't ever get that close to him again.

I was too old for him anyway. And falling for a heart-breaker would only make me look needy, and after forty, needy wasn't a good look.

"If you have any questions or anything, you can call me. All of the information should be in the file." I wanted Lilith to know that I cared about the job and had done my best to prepare for the event.

"The only thing I couldn't find was the menu, but since Jeffrey's here, I'm not worried about it."

I glanced at the single sheet of paper in my passenger seat. "I have the menu with me. Mr. Carpenter also has a copy." Hoping to smooth things over with Lilith—not that she seemed the least bit mad—I reiterated my promise to relocate to the small town nearest the venue. "I told you I'd move to Stadtburg, and I'm trying, but the only apartment complex in town doesn't have anything available right now. As soon as I find a place, I'll move, and then this won't be a problem." I'd stated in the interview that I was happy to move to the small town, hoping that would be a plus. Since I'd been hired, it had probably helped. Now I just had to make good on my promise. I didn't want Lilith to think I'd lied to her.

"I wish I could offer you a place, but the cabins on the ranch are full right now. But as soon as my stepson's friend decides she wants to marry him, one of the cabins should be available shortly after. I'm just not sure how long it will take her to realize that." A laugh bubbled out of her.

Her explanation didn't completely make sense, so I responded based on what I thought she meant. "I didn't know he was engaged."

"He's not. They're friends. Not even dating. He wants to be. Dating, I mean. And engaged. She's afraid of getting her heart broken, I think. Oh! The guys are here to help set up chairs. I'm not even sure how I got on the topic of Garrett and Tessa, but if you see them, it's best not to say anything. See you soon." Lilith ended the call.

I'd seen Garrett around, but I hadn't met Tessa. Protecting her heart was a good thing—healthy even—but I'd protected mine so long it was covered in cobwebs and probably growing mold. I kept it locked up tight for lots of reasons now. When I'd turned forty, I accepted that love wasn't going to happen for me. And I'd spent the last two years reminding myself of that. Daily.

Being stuck in the car with nothing but mocking brake lights in front of me gave me too much time to wallow in my own thoughts.

I boosted the stereo volume until the Red Hot Chili Peppers were so loud the car in the next lane could probably make out every word, but it didn't help drown out my thoughts. If the bull came into view, I'd turn the music down in case he wasn't a fan.

If Jeffrey was handling the food in my absence, it meant he'd be there when I arrived. Then he'd fill me in on all the details while I tried not to notice the sparkle in his green eyes and his hypnotic cologne. I wasn't even sure it was cologne or just the female-luring pheromones he gave off.

I gave myself a mental slap and reminded the part of my brain that kept thinking about Jeffrey of all the things I'd read about him. Granted, there were only three postings . . . from five or six years ago, but there was that saying about tigers and stripes. Or was it about leopards and spots? Anyway, the saying was true. Some men weren't capable of change.

Brake lights flickered, and traffic started moving. I eased onto the accelerator, and gradually, I moved forward. A red car with a huge dent in the passenger door sat on the side of the road, and a trailer blocked the inside lane. The wandering bull was now locked in the trailer, and he didn't look happy about it.

After starting my day like this, I hoped it would only get better from here.

THIRTY MINUTES before the first attendees were set to arrive, I turned into the main gate at the venue. After parking, I battled the seat belt to get it undone, then launched out of the car. Lilith was nowhere in sight, but Jeffrey was standing near the outdoor kitchen.

I hooked my purse on my shoulder, sucked in a deep breath, and marched toward him. As I approached the table, I started my explanation. "Thank you for covering. You'll never believe what snarled traffic."

He spun around. "Mindy, hi. I already—" He blinked, then turned back toward the table.

"A bull ended up on the highway. He dented a car, and then deputies and some cowboy who actually maybe knew what he was doing had to corral that bull into a trailer. It took them a while."

"A bull, huh? Things are set up. Cold stuff is chilled. Hot food is on the warmers. It should all be set." With his back to me, Jeffrey stared at the buffet table.

Of all the reactions I expected to my zany story, this wasn't one of them.

"Thank you for handling everything. I appreciate your help."

He gave a quick nod but didn't even glance at me.

Because things were awkward and my better judgment was still stuck in traffic, I continued to talk. "I hope this didn't interfere with your schedule. I'm really sorry."

"It's fine." Nothing on the table could be that interesting. The man was blatantly avoiding me.

I stepped up beside him. "This won't happen again. I'm embarrassed it even happened today."

"Traffic. Bulls." The normally charming and chatty Jeffrey was handing me short answers. He was mad.

It wasn't my fault that a bull had plowed into a car. I'd done my best to get here on time. "I hope this won't cause a problem in our working relationship."

"Working relationship?" Lilith laughed as she walked up behind me. "That makes it sound like y'all have another type of relationship on the side. And just so you know, I don't have a problem with that."

I turned to face her. "I'm so sorry I'm late. And Jeffrey and I only have a working relationship. I think my being late—"

"The buttons of your blouse came undone. I'm guessing you didn't intend to leave that much open." She winked, then pointed toward the building where the offices were located. "Happens to me all the time. I have a stash of small safety pins in my desk."

My cheeks burned as I followed her to the office. Jeffrey wasn't avoiding me because he was mad. It was because I was exposing myself. Accidentally. Horror coursed through me. What if he thought I'd done it on purpose? Now I had to work harder to make sure he knew I wasn't throwing myself at him.

Lilith pulled open the door for me to enter first. "I forgot to mention on the phone. I hired a helper. She'll be an extra set of hands around here. As long as she can keep them off the ranch hands." The information about my helper was starting to scare me. "Tandy has been asking if I have any openings. She's great with people, and I'm joking about her touching the ranch hands. Besides, they aren't over here much. But you'll understand when you meet her. She'll be here in about fifteen minutes."

All I needed was some boy-crazy teen hanging around while I was trying to run an event. What was Lilith thinking? But she was the boss, and I'd deal.

CHAPTER 4

JEFFREY

I tried to shove thoughts of Mindy's wardrobe malfunction out of my head as I stared at the blueprints laid out on my desk. Having plans drawn up for the expansion before I could justify the cost would only serve to drive me slowly insane, but that didn't stop me from pulling them out at least once a week and dreaming about the next phase.

My sister's idea to open a restaurant at her winery had changed everything. Pairing fine dining with the winery's beautiful setting drew lots of customers. My food brought them back again and again. If word continued to spread, I'd be able to break ground on the expansion hopefully next year. I just needed someone with a bullhorn or a massive following on social media to shout my praises. Was that too much to ask?

When my phone rang, I checked to see who was calling before swiping to answer. "Lilith, hi. What's up?"

"I had the section of fence fixed, so whenever you have time, we can move the bull over. People are going to love getting their pictures taken with a longhorn."

"I'll check with Mad Dog, but we should be able to do it one day this week. And while the bull is docile, he's not harmless."

"No man is." She laughed, then stopped when I didn't join in. "I thought it was funny."

"I just want to be clear about the bull."

"Jeffrey, my husband owns a cattle ranch. I know bulls are dangerous." The defensive edge in her voice amused me, but laughing would only make her mad. And no one wanted to make Lilith mad.

Shoot. I'd prefer to live my whole life without making any woman mad. Ever. Sadly, I had a talent for irritating those of the female persuasion.

"Good. Well, we'll take him over. You want us to put him in the small pasture or the bigger one?"

"Let's start with him in the small pasture. That way everyone can meet him." Her nails clicked on the desk. "And I have another question. Hear me out and don't get mad."

Now my defenses were up. "What a horrible way to introduce a question. I would've thought maybe Beau taught you that."

"Do you want to hear the question or not? I'm trying to help someone."

"I'm listening."

"This is a multipart question."

I dropped into my chair, quashing my irritation at the long, drawn-out buildup. "Okay."

Her deep inhale and quick exhale set me on edge.

"Are you interested in Mindy?"

"Excuse me?" My personal life was no one's business but my own. "Is this middle school? Who do you like? Please check the box."

"I told you not to get mad. My next question hinges on the answer. That's the only reason I asked."

"I have no plans *whatsoever* to ask Mindy out." I raked my fingers through my hair. "I guess all those years of being childish earned me these questions."

"We know you're a good guy. I just wanted to know because . . ." Her nails started clicking again. "At your place—correct me if I'm wrong—you have another house."

Where was Lilith headed with this line of questioning? And why did it feel like a stone had been dropped into my gut?

"The old house? Stephanie lived there while her place was being built, but she moved out months ago. Why?"

"So it's vacant?"

"*Why?*" I rubbed my forehead while I waited for her to answer. The headache beginning to pound on my skull had everything to do with her questions.

"Mindy needs a place to live. She tried to get a place in Stadtburg, but the only complex there is full. Goldie, Tessa, and Garrett are living in our three cabins. Well, Tessa isn't living there, but one of the cabins is hers. It's complicated. Anyway, I can't have Mindy live with the ranch hands."

I pictured Mindy walking to her cabin, being gawked at by the young ranch hands. Some of them were even her age. The image soured my stomach.

Lilith continued, "If you were interested, then it could be weird for her to live on your ranch, but since you're not, it seems like a great solution."

"Let Mindy know I have a place. If she likes the idea, have her talk to me." I'd put the offer out there and let Mindy decide.

"Perfect. You're a gem, Jeffrey. She'll be thrilled." Lilith ended the call without the slightest clue I'd lied through my teeth.

I didn't want to be interested in Mindy. She was nothing like the other women I'd dated except that she was much younger than I was. Most of my exes were short, barely cleared my shoulder. Not Mindy. Her height fell short of mine by maybe a mere five or so inches, which was tall for a woman.

But my entire body buzzed with attraction whenever she came near me. Thankfully, the other house was on the opposite side of my very wide driveway. That would be enough distance to avoid a constant buzz.

The house needed a good cleaning before I could let Mindy see it. I had a few hours until I needed to get dinner prep started, and since I wasn't sure when Lilith would mention the house to Mindy, I shouldn't wait to get it cleaned. As I strode out to my truck, I called my cleaning lady. Hopefully, she would work me in if I offered her double her normal charge.

While my cleaning lady made the house sparkle, I emptied closets of the stuff Stephanie had left behind. I'd never planned on having someone stay here. After moving the boxes into one of my guest rooms, I left instructions about closing up, then hurried toward the winery.

Stephanie met me outside the restaurant. "What's all the talk about clearing my stuff out of the house? Is it in your way?"

"Someone I know needs a place to stay." I pocketed my keys. "I packed up the stuff you left. If you don't have room for it, I'll keep it for a while."

"*Someone?*" My sister crossed her arms and lifted those dark brows. "Let me guess. She's young and short and giggles when you talk. I'm surprised you're even going to the trouble of pretending she'll be staying in the old house." If anyone knew how to push my buttons, it was my only sister, my younger sister.

"I'm reformed, remember?" I nodded toward the restaurant. "Follow me inside if you want, but I need to get started."

"I'll believe you've reformed when you stand at the altar."

"I'm not opposed to that idea. But every woman who would meet with your approval probably is opposed, and therein lies the problem. Just let me know what you want me to do with the boxes."

"Bring them by my place." She touched my arm. "But seriously, is she short and giggly?"

"The exact opposite of that, but she's only staying in the guesthouse. There is *nothing* else going on."

Stephanie grinned. "I knew it was a woman." Ponytail swinging side to side, she marched away, clearly proud of herself for getting information I hadn't intended to volunteer.

What had I gotten myself into?

CHAPTER 5

MINDY

*I*t was a good thing I'd worn my comfortable heels. I'd easily clocked five thousand steps during the event, and now that it was over, I kicked off my shoes and dropped onto the sofa in our little lounge area.

Lilith checked her phone as she settled into the easy chair. "You did a great job today. You didn't let the frustration of this morning affect you, and that's impressive."

"Thank you." I patted the couch when Tandy walked in. "I'm so glad you came today. You were a huge help."

Tandy grinned and plopped down at the other end of the sofa. "I'm just here for the view." She wiggled her eyebrows as Lilith's husband, Beau, walked around the corner.

"Y'all look worn out." He leaned down and kissed Lilith.

Lilith pointed at Tandy. "Behave."

Tandy let loose a belly laugh. "But that's no fun."

Beau shook his head. "Call me if you need me, Lily. I'm headed into town to pick up a few things."

"More Christmas shopping?" Lilith cocked her head.

"Yep." Grinning, he strolled out of the room. "But you have to wait until Christmas."

"We'll see about that." She leaned around her chair, watching as he walked down the hall. "Love you."

Tandy pushed up off the sofa. "Ladies, it's been fun, but I have a few chapters to write, so I'm headed home. Thanks for letting me come over and play."

"I'll call you again if you're interested," Lilith said.

Tandy pointed at her. "Call me."

As Tandy walked into the hall, Lilith turned to face me. "Good news! I found you a place to live. It's super close."

"Oh? That is great news." After the morning I'd had, living in a barn wouldn't be quickly dismissed as a possibility. "Where?"

"Jeffrey has a guesthouse that's not being used."

Were there any barns available? Living with cows, horses, or even goats would be better than living in Jeffrey's guesthouse.

Somewhere down the hall, Tandy laughed. "Oh, what fun!"

Living anywhere near Jeffrey didn't sound like fun at all.

Lilith peeked down the hall, then leaned forward when the door closed. "And I talked to Jeffrey about it. Just to make sure it would be okay. But I wasn't too worried because you aren't really his type, so you don't need to worry about it being weird or anything."

"That's a relief. I wouldn't want it to be awkward." It would be completely awkward.

"Around here, we all give him a hard time. He tried to move in on Joji before Clint came to his senses." She stood and stretched. "Anyway, if living there appeals to you at all, get in touch with him. I figured you'd be thrilled."

"Yeah. I guess he lives close to here?"

"Very close. You could walk."

Lilith was trying to be kind and helpful by finding me a place to live. And after she'd made a point to tell me I wasn't his type, I kept my mouth shut about all the reasons it would be a bad idea. Living in his guesthouse would only be awkward if I made it that way.

"Sounds great. I'll try to talk to him soon. The restaurant is probably serving dinner by now."

She nodded. "Yep. You're welcome to come hang out at the house for a bit if you want to delay driving back to your place."

"If I leave now, traffic shouldn't be too bad. But thanks." I stopped at my desk long enough to collect my purse.

There was a good excuse not to talk to Jeffrey today, but I couldn't put it off for long. Besides, every day I delayed was another day I had to fight highway congestion and risk having a bull stop traffic altogether.

IN MY APARTMENT, I kicked off my shoes as soon as I walked in the door. "I'm home, Sir."

Sir Lancelot swished his sleek gray tail as he strolled up the hall.

"Did I wake you?" I scooped him up and carried him to the kitchen. "We're going to be moving. Unless a certain chef doesn't allow cats in his guesthouse. Maybe he hates cats. Then I wouldn't have to live there."

"Meow."

"I'm glad you think so. Want the good stuff today?" I set him near his bowl and opened the cabinet where I stashed his cans of pâté. "I nearly died of embarrassment today. And that would've been bad because then who would come feed you?"

He started purring as I leaned down to put the food in his bowl.

"I love you too." I was a forty-two-year-old woman who

spoke to her cat as if he were a real person. I'd become a stereotype.

While he scarfed down his turkey pâté, I unbuttoned my blouse as I walked into my bedroom, reliving the horror of learning my red lacy bra had been visible to the public. Honestly, it wasn't such a big deal that Lilith had seen it.

Jeffrey was another matter altogether.

I definitely wouldn't be wearing lace when I went to talk to him tomorrow. Or anything with buttons.

Once I had on leggings and a sweatshirt, I opened the fridge. Normally, I loved cooking dinner. Mixing vegetables and seasonings and sometimes pairing it with seafood was how I passed the time on most of my weeknights. It was a never-ending quest to make something delicious that made up for all that I couldn't eat. While the food I made was tasty, I continued experimenting, hoping to make it even better.

But tonight, I didn't feel like cooking. I wanted to curl up with something hot to eat and a book to read and escape from reality for a few hours.

In the freezer, I found a heat-and-eat meal. After popping it into the microwave, I rested my head on the counter while I waited.

My phone buzzed at the same time the microwave dinged.

I swiped to answer before dragging the container out of the microwave by the edge of the packaging. "Hello."

"Mindy, hey! I got your message about the new job. It sounds great." Debra sounded as chipper as always, even more so now that she was married.

"I'm liking it. It's a change from what I was doing, and I might even be moving to that area. It's just west of San Antonio."

"A new job and moving? That's not going to change the

Christmas plans, right? We haven't gotten together in forever. I want to see you."

It had been less than a year, which was just shy of forever. But I missed my friends.

"I already mentioned my trip to my boss. She said being away at Christmas wasn't a problem. But I have to go home the day after because there is a big New Year's Eve party planned, and I'm in charge."

"As long as you'll be here for Christmas. That's what matters. Three weeks! I'm so excited." A voice sounded in the background. "I need to run. My honey's here, and he showed up with wine and flowers. I'm so lucky."

"Enjoy your evening." I was happy my friends had found love. Truly.

Four of us from college had stayed close, but then each of my friends found their special someone and one by one they'd gotten married. Our get-togethers had spread further apart, and some years, we only saw each other at a wedding and associated festivities. Like last year for Debra's wedding. They were all married now, and never again would I have to be a bridesmaid and endure all the nudges and comments about how I'd eventually get my turn.

All the people who'd said those things had been very wrong.

THE NEXT MORNING, Sir Lancelot jumped onto my bed and flopped down in the center of the quilt. He took advantage of the hours I was at work and deposited his gray fur on every square inch of the bed.

I'd already changed clothes four times, something that could be filed under not being awkward. "What about this, Sir? Does this look professional and like I'm not the least bit interested? I hope so because I don't have time to change again. Be good!" I tugged at the hem of the turtleneck. In this outfit, I couldn't be accused of flaunting anything. The soft fabric covered most of my upper body, excluding, of course, my hands and face.

With my purse hooked on my shoulder, I locked up my apartment and hurried down to my car. There weren't any events today, so I'd be mostly uninterrupted, but before the restaurant started serving, I'd go over and talk to Jeffrey.

It was silly to be nervous, and I hated that I was excited to see him again.

But I needed a place to live that didn't involve a forty-minute commute.

CHAPTER 6

JEFFREY

*M*indy hadn't called, and I was starting to wonder if she disliked me so much she'd rather endure an hour commute each way. I didn't know where in San Antonio she lived, but it was easily an hour to downtown.

I shoved those thoughts aside and tried to focus. Dinner prep was just starting. The restaurant had several reservations for tonight, and I'd be visiting a lot of tables and shaking a lot of hands. I'd learned pretty quick after opening that people liked meeting the owner and chef, so I split my time between the kitchen and the dining room. My well-trained staff handled things when I wasn't cooking.

If my happy customers would each tell a hundred friends, I might not have to wait months and months before breaking ground on the expansion project. I needed a blogger to shout my praises. People listened to them. Sadly, I didn't know any bloggers.

How strange was it that, at my age, I spent time each week checking out influencers on social media, hoping my name would appear? Well, not my name exactly. In the restaurant world, no one called me Jeffrey Carpenter. I was known as the Cowboy Chef. I hadn't chosen the name, but I loved it just the same.

But my awesome moniker had done nothing to help me win over the ladies. At least not since I'd chosen the straight and narrow.

One of tonight's specials featured my secret spice combo, and I always mixed it myself. Secrets only stayed secret if no one else knew. With the array of spices lined up in front of me, I portioned out what I needed and began measuring.

My assistant walked up beside me. "Mr. Carpente—"

I held up a hand. "Wait over there. I'll be with you in two minutes." Stopping in the middle of the portioning invited error. And I wasn't about to ruin tonight's batch. Once the spice was perfect, I strolled across the room as I wiped off my hands. "What's up, Laurel?"

"There is a woman here to see you."

"I'm not expecting anyone." It was early for dinner, so she surely wasn't here to eat. "Does she have an appointment?" I usually remembered what was on my calendar.

"She doesn't have an appointment, and she's not here for dinner. She wants to talk to you. I forgot to ask her name. She's tall, blonde." Laurel quirked an eyebrow, saying with her expression what she didn't with her mouth.

Not many women stopped by to see me, at home or at the office, and that made this visit interesting to Laurel.

I knew exactly who wanted to speak to me, and seeing Mindy again wasn't going to make concentrating on dinner any easier. "Thank you. I'll meet her in my office." Before leaving the kitchen, I made sure all the employees knew the menu and what they were supposed to do.

Then I walked to my office, much less sure about what I was supposed to do. Offering Mindy a place to live was risky for two reasons. She didn't like me. And I was attracted to her even though I tried not to be.

I'd repeatedly told myself that having Mindy in the guesthouse wouldn't affect our working relationship, but thanks to Lilith's comment yesterday, the phrase "working relationship" made me think of other kinds of relationships. And then my thoughts jumped back to the button mishap. How hard would it have been to say the word button? To calmly point out that it—and a couple of others—were undone? Instead, I'd stared at metal serving dishes, trying to think of words. At the time, only red and lace had come to mind, and I'd known better than to say that.

I had a reputation for being smooth and charming. Around Mindy, those skills withered.

She stood as I walked through the door, a professional and polite smile plastered on her face. She wore a vibrant blue turtleneck and jeans. There wouldn't be any button mishaps with that outfit, but it did show off her figure, which was the most unhelpful thing I could be noticing.

"Hi." I moved to the other side of my desk because a little distance was good.

"Thank you again for cove—I mean, handling—the event setup until I arrived. I spoke with Lilith about compensating you for the extra work." Mindy squared her shoulders and looked me in the eye.

"No need." Being over six feet tall, I was used to looking down at women, but Mindy had to be almost six feet tall herself, and it made for a different dynamic.

I wouldn't have to lean over to kiss her. A simple dip of my head would close the gap. Thinking about kissing her was counterproductive to squelching my attraction.

"Well, thank you." She inhaled, then blew out a breath. "Lilith mentioned you had a place available I could rent."

"My guesthouse is empty. Well, it's partially furnished but

not occupied. You're welcome to stay there." I pointed at the chair she'd vacated when I'd walked in. "Please. Have a seat."

She eased into the chair. "I'm not asking to be your houseguest, Mr. Carpenter. I'm looking for a place to rent."

"That's fine." I sat down. "I can't leave the restaurant right now. Tonight is going to be busy, but I'll message my ranch foreman. He can meet you out there and give you a tour of the guesthouse if you'd like to see it. His name is Mad Dog."

She sucked in a quick but silent breath, and her shoulders tensed.

I bit back a laugh at her expression. "He was the local pastor before he started as my ranch foreman. The nickname is a tad misleading."

Mindy visibly relaxed. "Oh, good to know. What time should I plan to meet him out there, and how much is the rent?"

"See if you like the place, and we can talk details tomorrow morning or whenever you have a few minutes." I checked the time. "As much as I'd like to do that now, I need to get back into the kitchen." My attempt to avoid any hint of flirting made me sound curt and uninterested.

"Of course. Sure. I'm sorry I bothered you at such a busy time. I wasn't really thinking about how you . . ." She stood and white knuckled her purse as she stepped toward the door. "I'll connect with Mad Dog and leave you alone."

"Mindy."

She stopped but didn't turn around.

"Here's Mad Dog's number. I'll let him know to be expecting your call or text. Getting to my place is easy. Go back toward the venue, continue another mile down that road, then turn into the gate on the right. That's my ranch." I moved around the desk and handed her the number I'd scribbled down.

She spun and accepted the note. "Thank you."

I really needed to say goodbye and get back to work, but my mouth had other ideas. "If you'd like to come back, my table is available this evening. Dinner will be on the house."

Something that didn't look anything like gratitude flashed in Mindy's blue eyes. "That's probably not a good idea."

She was right. Inviting her to anything that even resembled a date was a horrible idea, but that didn't keep me from asking another question. "Why is that?"

After hooking her purse on her shoulder, she crossed her arms. "I'm not sure you have anything on your menu I can eat. Most of what you make is rather . . . primitive. And also, I want to keep things professional." The woman couldn't just decline my invitation, she had to insult my cooking.

"Right." I tapped out a text to Mad Dog, hoping she couldn't read my shock. My anger, I didn't even try to hide.

Me: Possible tenant will be calling or texting about staying in the guesthouse. Please give them a tour.

"I've let my foreman know you'll be in touch." I slipped past her. "Can you find your way out?"

"Mr. Carpenter, I just meant—"

"You were quite clear, Miss Lawrence. Let me know when you want to discuss rental details." I didn't wait for an answer. I had primitive food to make for tonight's dinner guests.

Fighting my attraction should be a bit easier now.

CHAPTER 7

MINDY

*P*rimitive? What was wrong with me? I hated having to explain to people what I could and couldn't eat. Texas wasn't a popular place to say you didn't eat meat. It wasn't because I didn't like it. I couldn't have it, and to say I was bitter was an understatement. And based on what I'd seen of the food catered to the venue, meat was all Jeffrey ever made. Quite possibly because that was all that people ever ordered. Why hadn't the thought occurred to me in his office before that unkind word tumbled out of my mouth?

Now I owed Jeffrey another apology. I'd tried to take back what I'd said, but he clearly didn't want to hear it. I couldn't blame him. It was downright mean, and I hated that I'd said it. But at least I didn't have to worry about him charming me now. He'd probably never speak to me again. This would make our professional relationship awkward, and it had been my doing.

And he was going to be my landlord. I'd forgotten to ask about Sir Lancelot, so he could rescind the offer. It was just as well. If he'd changed his mind about renting the place to me, he could use my cat as an excuse.

My talent for putting my foot in my mouth could only be described as masterful. I never meant to come off as a . . . not nice person, but I stumbled into that persona often. Living with my walls up had earned me that sort of label more than once. How was I supposed to get Jeffrey not mad at me and still keep myself from noticing how the sprinkling of silver at his temples gave him a distinguished look? Or how broad and muscular his shoulders were? Or how well he fit into his Wranglers?

If he'd been the cowboy walking past my window on the interstate, I might've caused a secondary traffic jam when I rolled down my window and stared, oblivious of the other cars.

While I wanted to rest my head on the steering wheel and sob right there in the parking lot, I couldn't. With my luck, Jeffrey would walk outside and see me. Then he'd think I was an emotional mess. And he wouldn't have been wrong, but that was a secret I hoped to keep from the rest of the world.

Instead, I called the number he'd given me.

After three rings, a man answered. "Hello."

"Hi. This is Mindy Lawrence. I was trying to get in touch with Mr. Mad Dog."

"It's just Mad Dog. How can I help you?" His voice was kind, which was welcome after I'd put my foot in my mouth.

"Mr. Carpenter gave me your number. I'm interested in renting the guesthouse." After a second of silence, I added, "He said he texted to let you know I'd be in contact."

Another second of quiet had me worried I'd called the wrong person or said the wrong thing.

"Sorry about that. I hadn't seen his text. But yeah. I'm around. When do you want to come by?"

"Is now okay?"

"Yep. Need directions?"

"Jeffrey, I mean, Mr. Carpenter told me how to get there. I'm just leaving the restaurant." I looked up in time to see Jeffrey walk out the side door.

He had a phone pressed to his ear and was raking his hands through his hair. It was dark and thick. I laced my fingers together, imagining how those strands would feel.

With a blink, I tried to rid my mind of those thoughts. He had a reputation. I needed to remember that.

After another quick glance at Jeffrey, I drove back toward the venue and continued down the road. He'd called the place a ranch. Lilith hadn't mentioned that part, but it made sense with his moniker being the Cowboy Chef.

Just shy of a mile past the venue, a paved driveway came into view on the right, and I pulled through the gate, then followed the driveway until I saw what I guessed was Jeffrey's house.

On the opposite side of the driveway was a clapboard house painted a happy shade of blue. A walkway led off the driveway toward what must be the front of the house, which faced away from Jeffrey's house.

A man, who seemed familiar, walked up as I stepped out of the car. Grinning, he extended his hand. "Mad Dog Miller. It's nice to meet you."

"Hi. I'm Mindy Lawrence." I pointed at the quaint blue house. "I'm guessing that's the guesthouse."

"Yep. It's actually the older residence. The original cabin was torn down years ago, but this was the main house for a long time. Jeffrey's sister lived here for a while, but she moved out months ago." He pulled keys out of his pocket as he strode toward the side door, which was right off the driveway. "It's probably dusty because no one has stayed here since she left."

"He doesn't rent this place? I mean, normally."

Mad Dog pushed open the door and stepped aside for me to enter. "You're the first."

That remained to be seen.

Scents of citrus and pine hung in the air, and the place was immaculate.

"I was wrong. It appears this was recently cleaned. I guess Jeffrey handled that. Let me give you a quick tour." Mad Dog waved a hand, motioning to the counters and cabinets surrounding us. "This is the kitchen. It's been updated since the house was built, so there is a double oven and a dish-washer. The stovetop range is gas."

I followed as he continued into what was clearly the dining room.

"This is the only room that still has furniture, but if it's in your way, you can talk to Jeffrey about moving it."

In the middle of the room was a farmhouse table. There was a bench on one side and chairs on the other. Against the wall was a sideboard made of the same wood.

"They're beautiful."

"It's made of mesquite. The wood is from right here on the ranch. Jeffrey's grandfather—the Rodriguez one, not Carpenter, ironically—made these. Jeffrey has a similar set in his dining room." He continued into the living room.

"You seem to know a lot about not only the ranch, but the family."

"I've known Jeffrey since high school. I spent lots of hours in this house during the summers I was in town."

"Oh, I didn't realize you were such good friends. He'd mentioned you'd been a pastor, and I thought . . ." There was no way to finish that sentence without sounding rude, but after the stuff I'd read, I didn't expect Jeffrey to be good friends with a pastor.

Amusement crinkled near Mad Dog's eyes. "He's not so bad as people make him out to be. Bedrooms are back this way." His phone buzzed, and he glanced at it. "It's Ava, my wife. Have a look around. I'll be back inside in a few."

"Take your time."

He stepped out onto the front porch, and I wandered into the large room along the back of the house, which had been added after the house was built. There were more windows in this room. The back wall was nearly all glass.

Those windows offered a full view of Jeffrey's pool and hot tub. At least since it was cold out, I wouldn't have to watch him swim in his pool. But the hot tub could be used year around. Dang it. Maybe he wasn't a fan of hot tubs. Perhaps it had been a free bonus when he put in the pool.

Right. I'd need to get curtains for this room.

"Sorry about that." Mad Dog shoved his phone in his pocket as he leaned against the wall. "This is a great room, isn't it?"

"It is. The light in here is wonderful." I sounded like a realty ad.

"Did you get a chance to see the bedrooms? One of them has a view of the rose garden. Jeffrey's mom could make anything grow, and he's kept her garden going for years. Roses and herbs are all he grows now."

I hadn't pegged Jeffrey as a guy who grew roses. The herbs made sense for a chef, but growing roses because your mom loved them made Jeffrey all that more attractive. I'd have to read the posts that blasted him again to remind my heart to keep itself in check. But I'd just had a former pastor tell me that Jeffrey was a good guy, or at least not as bad as people made him sound.

But none of that mattered because I wasn't his type. And being rejected once in a lifetime was more than enough.

The first bedroom was painted a butter yellow and had two windows. One looked out toward the pool, the other toward the front of Jeffrey's house. I wouldn't be staying in this room.

Mad Dog walked through the kitchen, then pushed open the door to the other bedroom. "This is the master. It has a bathroom just around that corner."

My focus zeroed in on the rose garden outside the window. It filled the yard in front of the house. The living room had to have a similar view, but I hadn't noticed.

"It's December, but there are roses everywhere. How are they not all dead?"

Mad Dog laughed. "You'll have to ask Jeffrey about that. I'm here to keep the cattle alive, not the roses."

Since Jeffrey now hated me, the chances of us chatting about his rose garden were about as good as my winning the lottery. And I didn't play the lottery.

"This house is beautiful. Thank you so much for taking the time to let me see it."

"No problem. If you're interested, just let me know."

"I'm definitely interested. But I have one question. What is the pet policy? Because I have a cat, an indoor one."

"I'll let Jeffrey know. One of us will contact you about meeting again."

"Perfect. Thank you." I took one last glance at the roses before going to my car. This house was perfect except for one major detail—Jeffrey Carpenter lived right next door.

ON MY WAY HOME, I stopped to get boxes and picked up a gourmet salad. Tonight, I would forget about everything related to Jeffrey, and I'd start packing my apartment while sipping a glass of wine.

As I shoved open my apartment door, a stack of flat boxes tucked under my arm and my salad balanced in my hand, my phone buzzed. Phone calls were rare. Life had been different before, but ever since my friends had dropped out of the single-forever club, calls from them were spaced farther and farther apart. They had husbands who took up their time, so my life was quiet.

Twisting, I reached into my purse. The cardboard flats slipped out from under my arm, and with all the grace of a sea lion on land, I tripped on the boxes and landed on my hip. That would leave a bruise.

The buzzing stopped before I managed to get back on my feet, so I hobbled to a chair, then checked the phone only to see a missed call from an unknown number.

Sir Lancelot sauntered up and rubbed against my leg.

"Hey, buddy. I'll fill your bowl in a minute. I need to make a call first."

Maybe Jeffrey was calling about setting up a time to discuss details. Bracing for a conversation with the man I'd insulted, I called the number back.

A woman answered. "Mindy? This is Tandy. Since you're moving in with Jeffrey, I thought you'd need help packing. I'm in town, and I'll bring wine."

My assumption about Tandy being a boy-crazy teenager was wrong. She was a boy-crazy older woman. I hadn't seen her touch any of the guys, but she'd engaged in conversation with any guy who was nice to look at. I couldn't fault her for that.

I'd given her my number in case she'd needed something regarding the venue. Having her call tonight was unexpected, but having company would be a nice change. And I could set her straight about the moving-in-with-Jeffrey part. But I wouldn't be having any wine. I'd be skipping it because I'd be taking something to ease the pain in my hip.

"Tandy, hi. I'd love some help."

"Text me your address, and I'll head that way." She

laughed. "I can't wait to hear about Jeffrey. That man is a looker. I've been waiting for some woman to snag him."

"We're not—"

The line went dead. Either the call dropped, or she'd hung up on me. Either was a possibility. While I waited for my new friend to arrive, I ate my salad. The greens and assorted vegetables only reminded me of what I'd said to Jeffrey. Primitive. I might as well have called him a caveman.

Being tossed over his shoulder wouldn't be so bad.

Living close to him was going to make my building attraction more difficult to handle. I was much too old to be fawning over a man.

Twenty minutes later, a knock preceded Tandy's voice. "It's me. I brought fajitas. And wine."

Now all my neighbors knew that too.

"Hi. Come on in. I ate already, but help yourself to whatever you need." It was easier to say I'd already eaten—which wasn't a lie—than to explain that I didn't eat fajitas. When I'd admitted that to others, they looked at me like I'd grown horns.

But, oh, did those fajitas smell good.

She dropped the bag of food on the table, then propped a hand on her hip. "I *need* to hear about Jeffrey. I've been tracking his success for years. I knew his mama. Beautiful woman. And nice. That man got those green eyes from his dad, but that amazing, sunbaked skin came from his mama. She was a Rodriguez." Tandy shook her head. "I'm rambling now. But both Jeffrey and his sister have done very well for themselves. And now he has you!"

"Actually . . ." I cleared my throat, stalling as I tried to figure out how much to say and what I could leave out. The whole part about my shirt being unbuttoned would get left out. "There isn't anything going on with me and Jeffrey. Our relationship is strictly professional. As far as moving . . . I'm moving into his guest house. I'll be renting from him. That's all."

"Smart woman. Living on his property is a great way to get close to him. I bet he looks amazing without a shirt. You'll have to give me a report."

The look on my face must've reflected the horror I felt because Tandy laughed.

"Kidding. That joke is always funny. Always." She slapped her knee. "Oh! The look on your face. I'm really not a crazy old woman. Old, yes. Crazy? Only a little. But all that about taking shirts off is pure fun. I write romance novels, and people might not remember me if I were a quiet older woman who behaved herself. What's the fun in that? Memorable, that's what I am."

I nod, completely at a loss for what to say.

She clapped her hands together and glanced around. "We should get started. We need to get all this packed up and figure out a way for you to snag that Cowboy Chef. Pour me some wine. I'm going to need it."

"Just packing. That's all." I winced. "I'm not interested in snagging anyone."

"What's wrong?"

"Nothing. I'm just happy being single."

She wiggled her finger toward my face. "First of all, you can be happy being single and still meet someone and fall in love. But that wasn't what I was asking. You made a face. What hurts?"

"My hip. I'm clumsy and sore from a fall. I'll be fine." I clenched my jaw as I lowered myself into a chair. If I didn't take something, I wouldn't get anything done tonight. "I should probably take a pain pill."

"Yes, you should. I'll get started." She shooed me toward my bedroom.

I'd fallen on this same hip last year, no thanks to my cat. I reached for the muscle relaxers because those would ease the pain. But I wouldn't be drinking tonight, and hopefully I wouldn't say anything embarrassing to Tandy. I filled a small cup with water, popped a pill in my mouth, and washed it down. That would more than take the edge off my sore muscles.

Tandy assembled boxes and grinned as I walked into the kitchen. "Where do you want to start?"

"Either the bookshelves in the living room or those cabinets in here."

She pointed at my hip. "You don't need to be reaching and squatting with that hip. You pack the shelves, and I'll tackle these cabinets." With her help, I'd make a good dent in packing.

"Just so you know, I have a cat." I eased myself down to the floor.

Laughter echoed from the kitchen. "You are much too young to be a cat lady."

That wasn't true. If anything, I needed to get a few more cats.

AFTER HOURS OF PACKING, Tandy hugged me before walking out the door. "You go take another pill and don't worry about Jeffrey or what he thinks of cats. It'll all work out." She tapped her head and then her heart. "I know these things."

If any local productions needed a meddling grandma role filled, Tandy fit the bill.

"I'll take another pill." I wasn't agreeing to any of the other stuff. "Thank you so much for your help."

"I'll check in with the ranch ladies. If they have a free night, we'll descend on this place and get it all boxed up." She squeezed my shoulder. "You'll love them."

I wasn't sure who she meant by the ranch ladies, and this close to Christmas, I didn't want to inconvenience anyone. "I'm sure they are all busy."

"Nonsense. See you tomorrow." She sashayed out the door.

Sir Lancelot emerged from the bedroom, where he'd been hiding all evening.

"Did she scare you? I've heard she has that effect on men."

A message popped up on my phone.

Mad Dog: Would 9am tomorrow morning work? At the guesthouse?

Me: I'll be there.

I turned off lights in the living room and kitchen before heading back to bed. It was probably too soon to be packing since Jeffrey and I hadn't discussed the details yet. Maybe he didn't want a cat in the house, or he might've changed his mind after I'd been so rude.

We'd gotten a lot of packing done. That part of the evening was a success. But I'd failed completely in my resolve not to think about Jeffrey.

After taking another muscle relaxer, I crawled under the covers, wondering if Jeffrey liked cats and if he still hated me.

I really needed to apologize again.

CHAPTER 8

JEFFREY

I hadn't gotten enough sleep to be up this early, but if we didn't move the bull now, we'd risk traffic. Out here traffic meant a single car.

Mindy was coming at nine, and I didn't want her to wait on me.

As my first sips of coffee sent much needed caffeine into my system, Mad Dog stepped inside. "A new houseguest, huh?"

"She's renting the guesthouse; she's not a houseguest. Those two things are completely different."

He shook his head as he poured himself a cup of coffee. "Same words, only the order differs."

"Whatever."

He grinned. "I'd give you a hard time, but she's not at all your type. She's tall and smart. And she has a cat."

"I added a pet clause." After closing the restaurant, I'd come home and typed up a simple rental contract.

"Pet claws. Ha. That's funny."

It was my turn to shake my head. "You've really mastered those dad jokes."

Mad Dog had been my friend a lot longer than he'd been my foreman, and he wasn't wrong about my type. Mindy was nothing like the women I'd dated in the past. After turning fifty, I'd grown a few more brain cells and changed my ways.

"Are you done not giving me a hard time?"

"For now."

"Good because we have a bull to move."

Mad Dog set his empty mug in the sink. "Already have the halter on him. Hopefully he enjoys his early-morning walk."

"Hopefully."

"And then you have to meet with your houseguest." Clearly, he wasn't done giving me a hard time. "You going to mention the texts?"

"Yep." I'd have felt very different about Mad Dog's teasing before the woman insulted my food. "Still trying to decide what to say."

There were reasons reservations for my restaurant were fully booked almost every weekend, and primitive food wasn't one of them. Comments about my reputation and prior dating habits were deserved. Derogatory remarks about my cooking were not.

Keeping things strictly professional with Mindy wouldn't be a problem. All I had to do to chill my attraction was think of one word. And thanks to Mindy's middle-of-the-night texts, I'd been thinking about that word a lot, which meant Mindy had been on my mind. The rest of the night.

With barely enough time for a shower, I didn't have time for a second cup of coffee before nine. I grabbed the small creamer I'd bought for her place and walked over to the guesthouse. I'd make coffee there. That was the one thing my sister had left that I hadn't packed. A coffee maker.

Mindy pulled in five minutes before nine. For the second day in a row, she was wearing a turtleneck. How many of those did she own?

She tugged at the hem of her shirt as she walked toward the house, and I opened the door and leaned against the frame. When she looked up, she stopped dead in her tracks.

Her expression made it clear she hadn't expected me to be here.

Getting the weirdness of last night dealt with first was the most productive way to handle this meeting. "Rough night?"

Confusion knitted her brows, and she reached up to touch her hair. "No. Why would you say that?"

Did she not remember texting me in the middle of the night?

I wasn't going to play games with her, as tempting as it might be. "Because you texted me late last night begging me to forgive you and then saying—"

"No." Her head whipped back and forth as she dug in her purse. "I don't even have your number. Mad Dog messaged me, and I . . ." She pulled out the phone and stared at it. Her face went pale. "And then I texted you at two in the morning. I'm so sorry."

After that look of horror, I couldn't rub it in. "Let's get through the details of the rental really quick. I still haven't done my workout, so I want to wrap this up."

She blinked but otherwise didn't move. Her gaze drifted down to my chest then back up.

If I were the slightest bit interested—correction, if I allowed myself to be interested—having her take notice of my build would've been an ego boost.

Eleven texts. She'd sent me eleven texts and didn't remember. Five times, she'd asked me to forgive her. Please was used enough times for it to qualify as begging. Then, just as I'd been tempted to forget about her insult, she'd sent another two texts ranting about my primitive food.

And I was choosing not to rub it in. That either made me the bigger man or stupid.

"Mr. Carpenter, I apologize for disrupting your night. I'm not even sure where or how I got your number. After midnight, things were kind of a blur. I don't want you to think that—"

"That when you're awake in the middle of the night, you think of me?" Clearly, I wasn't the bigger man.

Anger flashed in her eyes. "I was going to say that I didn't want you to think I was drunk. I wasn't, but never mind. I'm sure you don't care what happened." She scanned her phone, and it wouldn't be long until she saw where she'd texted Mad Dog around midnight asking for my number. He'd let me know about the oddly timed message.

Wide eyes and a sharp intake of breath marked the exact moment she made the discovery.

"Try me." I was a lot of things but not heartless.

After staring at the counter for half a second, she lifted her chin and speared me with her icy blue gaze. "I fell in my apartment and took some medicine to help my sore muscles."

What was it about this woman that tied me in knots? After what she'd said about my food, my attraction should've withered. But no.

Silence stretched into seconds, and she hugged her purse to her chest.

While I wanted to carry her to my couch so she could sit comfortably and not suffer any lingering pain from her fall, that was the wrong approach. Living across the driveway from each other would be much smoother if Mindy Lawrence hated me.

I was good at two things—cooking and making women hate me, and I put that second talent to use. "So when your inhibitions are gone, you think about me and my primitive food? Good to know."

Instead of the expected flash of anger, regret swirled in her eyes. "I don't think your food is primitive. That wasn't what I meant."

"Then, please. Please, please, please, please. Tell me what you meant to say." It wasn't an accident that I used five pleases, and I felt a little more like a jerk each time I said it.

"I don't eat meat, and everything I've seen you serve involves some sort of meat—beef, pork, chicken, or something. But I chose my words poorly."

"You don't eat meat?" That revelation caught me off guard.

"I'm a pescatarian." She rubbed her hand up and down one arm. While it was a tad chilly, it wasn't cold. Why was she shaking? And were those tears in her eyes?

"A pescatarian?"

"Someone who only—"

I'd had my share of comments from people who accused me of animal cruelty, and my defenses were up. And this woman's power to discombobulate me intensified my reaction. "I know what a pescatarian is. I just don't know why someone would choose to live that way." I motioned inside. "Go in. You're obviously cold."

She marched past me, and after stepping into the house, she whipped around and pointed at me, probably to give me a piece of her mind. But then she sniffed and looked over her shoulder at the coffee pot.

Knowing how to distract her might prove helpful in the future.

I moved past her without giving myself enough room and my arm brushed the front of her.

She lurched backward and bumped into the counter.

I was taking things from bad to worse, but bumping her

hadn't been intentional. "Coffee? I need a cup. Haven't had a second one yet, and I was up at all hours. Sorry if I'm a tad out of sorts." If I kept up this persona, she'd not only hate me, but she'd also want me dead.

"I'll take a cup." She dropped her purse onto the counter. "Mr. Carpenter, I mean, Jeffrey. Since we're going to be living so close to each other and working together at the venue, we should clear the air."

"What's there to clear up, Miss Lawrence? You think I'm a cliché. In more ways than one if I had to guess, and I think you are . . ." Telling her what I thought of her was a horrible idea. "It doesn't matter what I think. Creamer is in the fridge. I didn't know what kind you used, so I got a small one." I moved to the other side of the small island and slid the rental contract closer to her. "If all that sounds fine, sign it, and we're set. There is a pet clause in there for the cat."

She read over the one-page contract while I sipped my coffee. "This seems low for rent."

"I made up a number. There aren't a lot of rental places in the area to compare to. Do you want it or not?" I hadn't exactly pulled the amount out of thin air. There were other houses that had rented within a few miles of here, and I'd taken the lowest and chosen an amount even lower.

"I want it. Let me pay you for the first month." Her pen glided across the paper as she added her signature. Was it any surprise that she had beautiful penmanship?

Everything about her was elegant and graceful.

She held out a check. "Here you go. I was hoping to move within a few days."

I nodded as I accepted the payment, then stuffed it into my back pocket. "You okay?"

"I don't care what you think of me." That icy blue gaze was back.

"I was talking about your fall."

"Oh. Yes. My hip is a bit tender, but I'll be fine." She rubbed it, which drew my gaze.

Finding something else to focus on, I opened the door. "Oh, and Miss Lawrence, if you ever need to take that medicine while you're living here, please let me know so I can lock my door. Texts are one thing, but visits in the middle of the night would be awkward. And keep your cat out of my herb garden."

Feeling very much like the playground bully who pulled on girls' pigtails, I slammed the door, but not in time to avoid hearing her gasp.

The door creaked, and footsteps sounded behind me. "It's *you* that's primitive. You're a *beast*."

Mindy had a place to live, and there was no danger of this relationship ever being anything more than professional.

Why did success feel so horrible?

WORKING out was less about staying in prime shape and more about keeping myself physically and mentally healthy. Starting each day with a workout helped give me focus. Today, it wasn't working.

I pushed up off the floor after my set of push-ups and grabbed the bar to do a set of pull-ups. Instead of running through my mental checklist of what needed to be done today, my thoughts had been hijacked by a thin blonde with a sore hip. My snide remarks had irritated her just as I expected. But the fury in her blue eyes was maddeningly attractive.

I yanked my body toward the bar over and over.

Even if she didn't hate me, she was too young. I'd given up dating women that much younger than me.

"You won't be able to cook if your arms fall off." Mad Dog leaned against the wall and sipped his coffee.

"Just doing my regular workout."

"Right." He glanced outside toward the guesthouse. "I'm here if you want to talk. You were there for me when I had relationship issues."

"I don't have any *relationship issues*." I let go of the bar and grabbed a towel.

Mad Dog shrugged. "When I was trying to woo my wife, you were there to set me straight. I'm just saying that I'm willing to offer a listening ear."

"You needed help. You didn't ask your wife out on a date until after your wedding. That's a relationship issue. I have a tenant. Completely different." I dragged the towel across my face. "She's much too young for me, and she thinks my food is primitive."

"This should be interesting." Laughing, he turned and called back over his shoulder as he walked out of my garage. "If you need someone to taste new menu items, I'm happy to do that for you."

"I'm not changing my menu because of her." That narrowminded stubbornness was not how I'd gotten this far in the restaurant business, but that woman irritated me as much as she captivated me.

One minute, she was luring me in by begging for forgiveness, and then she stabbed me again with insults about my food.

The worst part was, the firebrand who faced me down in the guesthouse this morning was so different from the quiet professional who worked events at the venue. It was as if she saved that side of her personality just for me.

Lucky me.

After finishing my normal routine, I changed into my swimsuit. The weather was a bit cool for a swim, but the pool was heated. And the water always felt good after a workout.

Using up every last ounce of willpower, I didn't look at the guesthouse as I strolled to the edge of the pool. I didn't care if she saw me.

After a deep breath, I stretched my arms up over my head and dove in. The cool water washed over me, calming my scattered thoughts. There was no reason to let that woman get under my skin.

When I reached the opposite edge of the pool, I took a breath, dipped back under the water, and started another lap. As I swam back and forth, my thoughts settled, and I was more than ready to start my day.

I came up for air and wiped water off my face. When I spotted heels at the edge of the pool, I swiped at my eyes again. Mindy had changed clothes. Instead of a turtleneck and jeans, she was now wearing a pencil skirt, blouse, and a red coat.

Thinking that her heels made her legs look long and shapely was the opposite of helpful. My brain didn't care.

She glanced down at her buttons, and it wasn't hard to imagine what she was thinking about. "Um, excuse me. I hated to interrupt your swim—which seems very odd for such a cold day, but whatever—but I needed to know if there is any problem with having a moving truck drop my stuff off this weekend. I didn't want it to be inconvenient or anything."

She could be so considerate and nice, but it was deceptive. There was a zing coming.

I let my gaze slide up her long legs and thin torso until I was looking her in the face. "Anytime this weekend is fine as long as they don't block my truck in."

She countered my long look with one of her own, but since I was mostly submerged in water, she got an eyeful of my shoulders and arms. "Okay. Thanks. I just wasn't sure what your plans were. Maybe you intended to be entertaining ladies around the pool or something."

And there it was. The zinger. "Why? You want an invitation?"

She spun around and clicked away on those fiery red heels.

Lucky me, indeed.

I folded my arms on the edge of the pool and rested my chin there while she stomped away. When she reached the door of the guesthouse and glanced back at me, I waved.

She wasn't my biggest fan, and that would make the living arrangements interesting.

CHAPTER 9

MINDY

Good thing I measured the windows because after work, I'd be buying curtains. If that man swam every day, I'd need them. How in the world did he look that good in his mid-fifties? It was criminal.

I parked outside the office and gathered my coat and purse before running inside.

Lilith met me inside the door. "So?"

"The place is great. I signed the paperwork."

"Fabulous. Now, you head home and pack. I'm giving you the day off. Tomorrow and Friday too." She crossed her arms. "And we'll be over to help tomorrow night. We couldn't make schedules work for tonight."

"Y'all don't have to go to all that trouble."

She waved away my comment. "No trouble. I'll keep you filled in on details about Saturday's event."

I'd been excited about this job, but there was a sense of family I hadn't expected, which made it a hundred times better. "Thank you."

I drove back into town and picked up another salad. My time was better spent packing rather than cooking.

Sir Lancelot was happy to see me if the purring was any indication. He wasn't as happy that the tape gun made noises and that things in the apartment were moving around. He wasn't a big fan of change. We had that in common. I'd had enough change in my life, and most of the time, it hadn't made things better.

I spent hours packing, then when my hip ached, I dropped onto the sofa with a snack and searched for more incriminating posts about Jeffrey to help bolster my guard. Instead, I found posts about how he'd spent last Christmas cooking for a children's charity.

That information was the opposite of helpful.

I read through the texts I'd sent him, even more horrified now. As embarrassing as those messages were, at least I hadn't revealed more of my thoughts. He'd never let me forget it.

I wouldn't be taking that medicine again no matter how badly I hurt myself.

LILITH HADN'T BEEN specific about who was coming over to help me pack. Tandy had mentioned the ranch ladies, which probably included Ava. Then puzzle pieces clicked together in my head. Mad Dog seemed familiar because he'd shown up at the venue when I'd worked the event with Ava. He was her husband.

The folks out there were one happy little family, and they'd gone out of their way to make me feel welcome. If they liked Jeffrey, maybe my initial opinion of him had been wrong. But that didn't mean I'd throw myself at him.

Right at six, the time Lilith said they'd arrive, there was a knock.

Braced for questions about my new landlord, I pulled open the door.

Tandy, Lilith, Ava, and another woman, who was shorter than the other ladies, flashed wide smiles. Tandy rubbed her hands together. "We're here to help."

"Come in." I stepped aside. "I appreciate this."

The short woman stuck out her hand. "Joji Jackson. Pleased to meet you. I know what a pain moving can be."

"Thank you for coming. Do you live on the ranch as well?"

"Sort of. I own the goat farm that shares a fence with the ranch. Bought it from Beau. Then I married his ranch foreman." She wiggled her eyebrows. "I think the ranch has some sort of magic. Maybe it'll surprise you too."

"I guess we'll see." I forced a smile, quite sure there were no surprises in store for me.

She patted my arm. "I didn't expect it either. Now, tell us what to do. And do you mind if I play music?" She held up a portable speaker.

"I don't mind a bit." I told them what to leave out and where to stack the boxes, as if the growing stack in my living room didn't give them a hint.

Classic rock blasted through the speaker as the ladies set to work. The four of them worked as efficiently as a colony of ants. Within a short time, my kitchen cabinets had been emptied, all the contents packed up. Everything from my bathroom—except what I needed for the couple of nights—had been shoved into boxes.

The only things left in my living room were large pieces of furniture.

I stared at the stack of labeled boxes. "This is amazing. Thanks to y'all, all I need to do tomorrow is clean this place."

Tandy propped her hands on her hips. "And coax that cat out from under your bed. I don't think he likes me."

"He's a bit shy."

Lilith laughed. "Tandy's heard that line before."

Joji checked the time. "It's not that late. Why don't we go get dessert somewhere?"

Having help had been amazing, but enjoying company had been even better. Now that they were talking about getting dessert, I'd have to explain about my dietary restrictions.

Usually when I explained what I could and couldn't eat, people smiled politely and pulled away. Including me took extra effort, and I missed out on lots of social gatherings as a result.

Ava nodded. "I'm always up for dessert."

"Dessert and kisses. That's just about all I need to survive." Joji wiggled her skinny hips.

Lilith looked at me. "Will you join us?"

"I don't know. I have an allergy to gluten, so sometimes it's hard to find food I can eat in restaurants."

"Surely there's a place where you can eat something sweet. Let's see what we can find." Joji tapped away on her phone. "What about this one? It looks like they have ice cream and a few gluten-free options. This cookie thing looks amazing!"

I wasn't used to people going to so much trouble for me, and after she'd made the effort to search, I wasn't going to say no. "Sure. Let me grab my coat."

Ava hung back as the other ladies stepped outside. "I'm glad we were able to come over tonight. It's good to get to know you better. And if you ever need anything—at all—you can call me or Mad Dog or any of these ladies."

"Thanks."

"Or Jeffrey." She nudged me.

Calling Jeffrey for help was near the top of my things-not-to-do list.

We all loaded into Lilith's SUV and headed to the restaurant.

As soon as we were all nestled into a booth, Tandy leaned forward. "Are you excited?"

"I'm looking forward to living closer to the venue. That will make my commute so much easier."

"And on days when traffic is bad, he could always carry you over." She grinned.

Lilith shook her head. "Leave the woman alone, Tandy. She's not interested in the man."

Tandy picked up her menu. "If you say so. But I saw them together, and you know how those little heat waves radiate off the hood of a car? Yeah, that was definitely happening."

Ava snickered. "It's possible to just be friends, Tandy."

It was Joji's turn to laugh. "You proved that, Ava. Oh, wait."

Then all of them were laughing, and I was lost.

Lilith bumped my shoulder. "Ava married Mad Dog and insisted they were only friends. It didn't quite work out that way."

Joji pointed at Lilith and Ava. "The three of us all found love later in life. We haven't been married all that long. Lilith and Beau argued until they finally kissed. I wasn't around for that, but I've heard the stories. I was the sunshine to my cuddly grump. And Ava married Mad Dog to help him out of a bad situation. Sooooo, if you ever want to chat or ask advice, we're all willing to talk. Tandy is a retired sex therapist, so she's a good one to go to if that's what you want to discuss."

I slapped a hand over my mouth to cover my horrified laugh. As shocking as it was, Tandy as a sex therapist made sense, but it was still funny to me. "Thanks. If I ever meet anyone and need advice, I know who to talk to."

Tandy rolled her eyes. "You have met someone. But I'll be quiet for now. Where's that waiter? I need chocolate."

Lilith cocked her head. "You know, Tandy. I've never heard your story. I know you write romance novels and about your previous job, but what about relationships? Were you ever married?"

"You don't know because I've never mentioned it, and I don't intend to." She smiled as a young guy walked up with his ordering pad.

"Evening, what can I get you ladies tonight?" The waiter smiled despite the tired circles under his eyes.

We all ordered, and the conversation moved away from Jeffrey and onto other topics. But he'd come up again at some point, and hopefully, I could keep the ladies thinking I wasn't interested when it did.

CHAPTER 10

JEFFREY

Saturday morning, I rolled over and yanked a pillow over my head when the rumble of the moving truck engine woke me. After a very late night at the restaurant, I didn't want to be awake this early. I'd been shorted on sleep too often this week because of Mindy.

But staying in bed and grumping about life wouldn't make anything better.

I yanked on sweatpants and made a pot of coffee before texting Mad Dog. He never stopped by the house on Saturday mornings unless he knew I was up. Hiring him was the best decision I'd ever made. I no longer gave a second thought about the day-to-day operations of this place.

Standing by the back door, I scanned social media, checking out the influencers to see what restaurants had been mentioned. I really only wanted to know if my place had been talked about. Every few minutes, I glanced out and watched Mindy direct the movers. The three guys were almost comedic in the way they carried the boxes out of the truck in a single file line.

Based on the expression on Mindy's face, they were

trying her patience. That was a look I recognized. It had been directed at me more than once.

"Still hate her?" Mad Dog chuckled and grabbed a mug out of the cabinet.

"Never said I hated her."

"You like her then?" He filled his mug with black coffee, then leaned against the counter.

I winced as the moving guys dropped her couch. Her arms were in the air, and I was glad her lecture didn't penetrate the door. "Wouldn't say that either."

"For someone you don't like and don't hate, she sure is getting a lot of your attention." He stepped up beside me and looked out.

Mindy's gaze cut to my back door a moment, and then she followed the three stooges inside her house.

"She seems just as uninterested as you are." He downed his coffee. "I'm off to do ranch stuff. Have fun."

"I'm pretty sure she hates me."

"Probably." He picked up his hat off the counter and walked outside.

I looked out the back door again, and Mad Dog was strolling toward Mindy, who had walked outside.

I didn't need to stare. What I needed was a second cup of coffee and a workout, so I ignored Mad Dog's conversation with Mindy and went into the garage.

After working through my Saturday routine and skipping my swim because I didn't want to give my neighbor the opportunity to lob insults at me, I grabbed my keys. Anything was better than staying here right now.

I pulled open the front door, and Mindy's eyes went wide, her fist hovering in the air as if she were about to knock.

"Hi." She swallowed, which made me think bad news was coming.

"What's up?"

She crossed her arms. "There is a little bit of a problem."

I leaned out and looked toward the guesthouse. "What? Did they drop something else?"

As the words left my mouth, I wanted to kick myself. Now she knew I'd been spying on her. Not spying. Watching. But the word choice didn't make much of a difference.

"Only the couch, which survived. But they cut the corner when pulling out of the gate, and—"

I ran past her to see what those guys had done. If my very expensive fence had been damaged, someone would be paying for the repairs.

The truck sat angled at the end of the drive, blocking any possibility of leaving. And the two flat tires on this side sank any hopes of it moving soon.

Dragging my hands through my hair, I sighed.

Mindy stepped up next to me. "They called it in, and the company said someone would be out *soonish* to tow the truck. I'm sorry."

"Yep." I turned to head back to the house.

She ran to catch up with me, but there was no click because she didn't have on her pretty heels today. They'd been swapped for cute plaid tennis shoes. "Look, I didn't mean for this to happen. It's not good for me either. I'm supposed to be at the venue in thirty minutes. All my careful planning proved useless." She laced her hands on top of her head. "Lilith is going to think I'm the worst employee ever. First, I'm late because of a stupid bull, and now because of this truck."

For just a second, Mindy's tough exterior was gone, and even I, dense as I could be, sensed her panic. Then she blinked, and Mindy was her guarded self again.

But that panic was something I couldn't ignore. "Do you have a jacket?"

Mindy's brow furrowed. "In the house, but why does that matter?"

"Go get it. I'll take you to work." Since no good deed went unpunished, I knew my choice would come back to haunt me. "And don't change clothes."

She stared down at her outfit, and I made a point not to do the same.

"I can't wear this to work."

"Pack a bag and change there. Trust me." I crossed my arms, ready for her arguments.

"Trust you?"

"Is that so hard?"

She rolled her eyes. "You have no idea."

"I'll meet you right back here in a few minutes." I walked around the house and out to the barn.

Mad Dog glanced up as I opened the door. "Need something?"

"A horse. I'd like to take Beauty, but Beast will handle two riders better."

"I'll saddle him for you." He grabbed a Pillion saddle. "Two riders, huh?"

"Yep." I hoped Mad Dog wouldn't ask any more questions.

He worked quickly without saying another word, and I had Beast out front right as Mindy stepped out of her house.

She stopped when she looked up. "A horse?"

"The venue isn't far. Beast will have us there in no time."

"Beast?" Her eyebrows inched upward. "You didn't."

"Don't flatter yourself. He had his name long before I ever set eyes on you." I swung up onto the horse, then shifted to a spot where she had something to use as a step. "Just hop up behind me and hang on."

She handed me her bag, then climbed up behind me with all the grace I expected from her. "I'm ready."

"Wrap your arms around me."

Showing off her stubborn side, she crossed her arms again. "I'm fine."

"Have it your way." I nudged Beast, and he started walking. After another quick nudge, Beast shifted to a canter.

In an instant, Mindy had her arms around me, and her cheek pressed against my back. If I wasn't so set on not liking her, I might've liked the feel of her arms around me . . . more than I already did.

The sensation of having her body molded to mine wouldn't be easily forgotten.

.

CHAPTER 11

MINDY

When I spotted Tandy near the porch, I pulled my cheek away from Jeffrey's back, but I didn't let go of him. Galloping wasn't necessary, and I guessed he was doing that so I'd hang on tight. It was working.

I'd sworn never to be in his arms again, and technically, I wasn't. He was in mine. The effect was the same. I was chocolate. And he was the summer sun.

Tandy waved as Jeffrey steered the horse toward the office. I'd be hearing about this for the rest of the day. Maybe the rest of the year.

"Be still my heart. This is inspiring a scene for my romance novel. But in the book, the guy will be shirtless." She winked at Jeffrey. "Want to help me visualize that?"

He stopped the horse near the edge of the porch. "It's a bit cold for that, I think."

"That didn't stop you from going for a swim the other day." I still hadn't loosened my death grip on his middle, but now that the horse was stopped, I pried my fingers apart. And it was entirely possible the feel of his firm abs under his thermal pullover had me thinking about how he looked in a swimsuit.

He covered my hands with one of his, and I stilled. "Careful."

That caution could be applied to so much more than sliding off this horse.

"Ooooh! You've seen him without a shirt. You promised to give me a report." She rubbed her hands together.

I felt every bit of the insulting chuckle that rumbled inside Jeffrey.

"I never said anything of the sort." I directed my angry grumble at him.

"I believe you." He patted my hand. "You should be able to slide down onto the porch. But, like I said, be careful."

The contrast of the smugness and gentleness had me in knots, so I yanked my hand away. "I'll be fine." I swung my leg over the side and dismounted with more grace than I thought possible given how tangled I felt. And honestly, disliking him wasn't as easy now that this cowboy had given me a ride on his horse.

Standing on the porch, I grabbed my bag when Jeffrey held it out. "I'm sorry about the truck blocking your driveway. And thank you for the ride." Professional. That was my aim.

"Unless you slashed their tires, I can't really blame you." He stroked the horse's mane. "Will you need a ride home?"

"I'm sure I can figure it out."

Tandy laughed and pulled open the office door. "You should definitely come get her after work."

I waited until the door slammed behind me. "Ignore her."

Jeffrey leaned forward on his horse. "Well, as we've already established, you have my number, so if you need a ride . . . text me. Preferably before two in the morning." With a smirk, he sat tall in the saddle and turned his horse around.

"I already said I didn't need you."

Just when my defenses started crumbling, Jeffrey supplied the mortar to strengthen them once again. He was full of himself, and I'd do well to remember that.

He waved over his shoulder, then galloped away.

Avoiding Tandy and Lilith, I slipped into the restroom and changed into something more appropriate for work. Then I shoved my other clothes in my bag.

Living on Jeffrey's ranch was off to a bad start. Surely, it could only improve from here.

When I stepped into the building, Lilith smiled and crossed her arms. "Tandy is trying to convince me there is something sparking between you and Jeffrey. I was under the impression you couldn't stand the man."

I hated the implication from Tandy, but it horrified me that Lilith had picked up on my dislike of Jeffrey. I'd tried to maintain a cordial and professional relationship with him when we were at the venue. Apparently, I'd failed in keeping my distaste a secret.

"I have no issue with Jeffrey. He caters events here and is currently my landlord. Beyond that, we have no relationship." I shifted the bag to my other shoulder. "I'm sorry if at any point—"

Lilith rested a hand on my arm. "You wouldn't be the first woman to find Jeffrey smug and arrogant, but behind that persona is a genuinely good guy. As for Tandy, she thrives on drawing reactions from people. One day, maybe she'll get a taste of her own medicine, but until she does, we just have to laugh and let her be herself."

I nodded. "Thank you."

"And don't ever tell Tandy how Jeffrey looks without a shirt because she will hound that man to be on one of her covers. If you don't believe me, ask Beau. My poor husband avoids that woman. She saw a photo of him without a shirt and has hounded him ever since." Lilith lowered her voice. "I took the picture when I was still under the delusion he was smug and arrogant, but that's a story for another day."

I hadn't planned to tell Tandy how in shape Jeffrey was for a man in his fifties. Lilith's advice only added to my determination. But not telling anyone how he looked didn't stop me from thinking about it. Dang that man. Why did he have to work out daily? And worse, why did he have to deliver me to the venue on horseback?

It would be easy to fall for that Jeffrey, not that he'd invited falling of any sort. But then that smirk appeared. Even though I had his number, there was no way I was asking him for a ride home. I'd sooner walk. Uphill. In the snow.

Thankfully, I lived in Texas, and snow here was rare.

I LOVED the venue after an event was over and everyone had cleared out. It truly was beautiful out here, and without anyone else around, it was quiet. Beyond the cluster of buildings were grassy fields and trees. A river bordered the other side of the venue, and an open-air chapel sat nestled among trees not far from the bank. With the rippling of the water and the singing birds, this place was a sort of paradise.

The closest I'd ever come to living in the country was having an apartment that faced a greenbelt. Deer had wandered on the other side of the fence, and that was the sum of my experience with wildlife.

Riding the horse had been new and different, and when I unlatched a gate to cut through the field to get to the building on the far side, which seemed like a shortcut, I was thinking about the horse . . . and his rider. Mostly the rider. And that was why I didn't notice the large bull smack dab in the middle of the pasture until he picked up his head from the feeding trough. As soon as I spotted him, I froze.

Was I supposed to run, freeze, or scream? Doing all three wasn't physically possible, at least not at the same time. But because my body refused to move, I prayed the freeze option would keep me alive.

The long horns looked sharp and could probably poke a hole in my middle big enough to drive a Smart car through. Obviously, I didn't want that to happen.

This was bad. Both Tandy and Lilith were gone, and the cleaning guys were all inside the building on the far side of the venue. If I screamed, they wouldn't hear me. And if this bull didn't like my screaming, that could make this worse.

Why, of all the colors available, had I bought a red coat?

Afraid to turn my back on the massive beast that kept one eye fixed on me while he continued to eat, I slipped my hand into my pocket and grabbed my phone.

I tapped Lilith's name, but the call rolled straight to voice mail. I could be dead by the time she got the message. I couldn't imagine Tandy would be much help. There were only two other numbers I could call, so I dialed Jeffrey's foreman. Surely, Mad Dog would help me.

But he didn't answer his phone, so I dialed my last and worst option.

"Oh, Mindy, what a surprise to hear from you. Do you *need* me?" Jeffrey laid the tease on thick.

Keeping the panic out of my voice was a lost cause. "Please help me. I walked into the little fenced-in area, and—"

"Crap. Stay on the line. He shouldn't bother you, but . . ." Keys jingled. Then a truck engine rumbled to life. "I'm on my way."

"I'm wearing my red coat. If I stay still, you think maybe he won't notice?"

"Bulls are color blind. Stay still. That's what matters." He mumbled under his breath. "Why would you walk into a pasture with a bull?"

"I haven't seen anything in this field since I started working here. How I missed an animal this large is unfathomable, but can you please lecture me later?"

"I have your attention now, so it seems like a good time. What's Chuck doing?"

"Chuck?"

"The bull, Mindy. What's he doing?"

"Chuck as in roast?"

A full belly laugh came through the line, which might've made me smile except for the whole staring-death-in-the-face situation. "No, Chuck as in short for Charlie. But I really should've saved that name for a horse. Now, back to the part about what he's doing."

The truck came into view, speeding up the road.

"He's eating . . . and eyeing me." I kept my face turned toward the bull but looked to the side, needing to see that Jeffrey was really on his way.

"Just don't turn around, okay? Never turn your back on a bull." The truck stopped, and Jeffrey hopped out. "I'm hanging up now."

I nodded and dropped the phone into my coat pocket, listening as his boots crunched on the gravel, then landed more softly on the grass.

His hand pressed to my back as he stepped around me and positioned himself between me and the bull. "Hey there, Chuck. I see you got to meet Mindy." Jeffrey turned his head and whispered over his shoulder. "Stay behind me. We're going to walk backward toward the gate."

If by "stay behind me" he meant plaster yourself to my back, I did as I was told. When he moved, I matched his steps. Even terrified, I noticed the firmness of back for the second time today. It felt exactly as I'd imagined it would when I'd gaped from the edge of the pool as he glided through the water, but I'd eat a burger—which would likely land me in the hospital—before admitting any of that to him.

Jeffrey reached back and clasped my hand. "Chuck, she's not horrible. Trampling her would be a waste of energy, so if she ever wanders in here again—which I doubt she'll do—just ignore her. That's what I do most of the time."

Instead of wanting to hug him when my butt hit the gate, swatting him sounded more appealing.

He reached back and opened the latch without taking his eyes off the bull, then closed the gate once he was out. "Stay out of Chuck's pen. He's docile, but animals that big are always dangerous."

"I *get* that he's dangerous. I didn't *know* he was in there." I yanked my hand out of his and backed away, crossing my arms as I did and willing my body to stop shaking. "I'm not stupid."

"Hey." Jeffrey opened his arms and stepped closer. "That's not what I said."

Because my body had no regard for my brain at the moment, I leaned in and let him wrap me in a hug, a choice I knew I'd regret. "Thank you for coming so quickly."

For fifteen heartbeats, neither of us spoke.

"We moved Chuck over here from my place a few days ago. So far, his favorite spot seems to be between the barn and the tree. You've probably walked past him several times just today." There was no condescension in his voice. "You all done here? I can give you a ride before I head over to the restaurant."

Hugging this man was as dangerous as staring down a bull, so I pushed away from him. "I'm not done yet. I'll be here another hour or so. But thank you." I was still shaking a little, so I stuffed my hands into my coat pockets. "I vaguely remember something about Lilith asking if I'd met Chuck. I thought he was someone new on the cleanup crew."

"Sorry about the scare."

"Oh, I'm fine." I needed him to believe that lie so he'd leave. "Did they get the truck moved?"

"Yep. Otherwise, I'd have shown up on my horse." He eyed me a second before pulling keys out of his pocket. "How will you get home?"

"It's not far. I can walk. Conveniently, I have a change of clothes."

That smirk appeared again.

"All right, well, I'm off to go make my primitive food."

He'd never forget that, but it was just as well. Because if he decided to truly turn on the charm, I'd be a goner. My defenses had a Jeffrey-sized hole in them.

And that wasn't good at all.

CHAPTER 12

JEFFREY

J knocked as I pushed open Lilith's office door. "I think asking your employees if they've met Chuck is a horrible way to let them know there is now a bull on the property."

She blinked and pushed her readers up to the top of her head. "What are you talking about? Did Chuck hurt someone? You said he was docile."

"He is, but an animal that big is never safe. Everyone should have been informed. If anything had happened to her, I'd feel responsible."

"To her?" She cocked her head and leaned back in her chair.

I should've had a least one cup of coffee before storming in here. "I'm not accusing you of anything. Just make sure everyone knows to stay out of the pasture when he's in there. And Chuck should have a handler when people are around him. Always." I rolled my shoulders, still irritated but less so after delivering my lecture.

"I'll make sure everyone knows there is a bull on the

premises." She tapped a manicured nail on the desk. "Anything else you want to get off your chest?"

"No." I turned but stopped with my hand on the doorknob. "My assistant said you'd asked about reservations. My table is free all week. Just call and let her know what night you want to have dinner."

"Thanks, Jeffrey."

The amusement in her voice kept me from looking at her. After a quick nod, I slipped into the hall.

Mindy stood at the end of the hall with her fists on her hips. "Thanks for telling everyone about how stupid I am. It's greatly appreciated."

"Your name didn't come up." I brushed past her.

Her heels clicked behind me as I made for the exit. "After your little temper tantrum in there, everyone knows. *Her* isn't very vague. I'm the only other full-time employee. And I seriously doubt she thought you were talking about Tandy."

"I wouldn't want her hurt either, and there are people who clean up after events."

"Currently all of them are male." She sighed. "I want this job. But if . . ." After a glance back at Lilith's office, Mindy moved closer to the exit. "If I keep messing up, she won't keep me around."

"Lilith isn't going to let you go over this, and I promise to stay out of your way."

When I shifted to step around her, she moved to block my exit. "Jeffrey."

"What?"

"You wouldn't have been responsible. I'm the one who decided to take a shortcut."

"Okay." I needed air and coffee, but more importantly, I needed to be away from Mindy. She triggered all my old temptations, and I wasn't falling back into that. I wanted to see my name in posts because people liked my food, not because I had another young woman on my arm. "I need to go."

Unmistakable hurt shone in her eyes, but trying to smooth things over would only end up making the whole situation worse.

She flashed her professional smile, the one that wasn't completely fake but didn't bubble up from inside. "Have a good day."

I doubted that was possible.

After the short trek home, I downed two cups of coffee, then went out to the wood pile. Push-ups and pull-ups weren't going to cut it today.

A half hour later, I tossed another split log onto the stack and wiped my brow. The weather was cool and I was under the shade of a tree, but that hadn't prevented me from working up a sweat.

Mad Dog looked at his phone as he walked up. "That's a lot of firewood. I'm checking the weather. Are they forecasting a blizzard?"

"Funny. I'm just working out some frustration."

"What did she do now?" Mad Dog leaned against the tree. "Because from what I've seen, she's been an excellent tenant. The truck thing wasn't her fault."

"I'm not blaming her for that." I stood another log on end and brought the axe down, sending two pieces of wood tumbling. "She ended up in the pasture with Chuck yesterday. Didn't know he was there and was taking a shortcut through the field."

"Does that have anything to do with why she called me yesterday? I called her back and left a message, but I haven't heard from her since."

"I'm guessing I wasn't the first one she called, but I raced over when she did. I can only imagine how many people she called before me. But nothing happened. She was fine."

"But you keep thinking about the other possibilities."

"She was quaking, terrified. I hated seeing her so scared."

"So that's why you were in there ranting to Lilith this morning." Mad Dog tapped on his phone.

I loved having a group of friends, but I didn't like the rate at which news traveled. "Don't be texting Ava about this. How did you know I'd been over to talk to Lilith?"

"Ava." He stuffed his phone into his back pocket. "That's why I came to find you. The ladies are a bit concerned."

"There's no need. I'm fine." I chopped another log. "But if the ladies want to be helpful . . . Mindy could probably use a friend. She doesn't really know anyone around here. Except Tandy, but I'm not sure that's a good thing."

"Ava and the gang helped her pack the other night."

"Well, good."

"Anything else on your mind?"

"Nope." Not anything I wanted to share at least.

Mad Dog patted my shoulder. "Good. Now, put the axe down. Go for a swim, then get ready for work."

"You're probably right."

He cupped a hand near his ear. "What's that? I'm not sure I heard you."

"I'm not going to say it again." I strode ahead of him. "For the record, I don't want to talk about Mindy with you or anyone."

"Got it, boss."

A conversation with him had done more to clear my mind than all the wood I'd chopped. Now that I knew Mindy had friends and support, I didn't have to think about her anymore.

She had a good job, a place to live, and a group of friends ready to support her. She didn't need me.

~

NOT THINKING about Mindy would be a whole easier if she weren't standing at her back door peeking out the side of her curtains while I swam every morning. Did she think I wouldn't notice the coffee cup catching the light every time she took a sip?

I had upped my lap count and added a few stretches to the routine I did before diving in. And the part of my brain I shared with my fifteen-year-old self hoped she was impressed. The more logical side of my brain said I shouldn't care what she thought.

I yanked the towel off the back of the lounge chair and dried my face before toweling off the rest of me. The weather had warmed up, too hot for Christmastime in my opinion, but because of that, I wasn't fighting the cold while showing off.

But the most interaction I'd had with Mindy in the last two weeks was a wave across the driveway. It had done little to douse my spark of attraction, and I hovered a hair above grumpy most days.

And two days before Christmas was a bad time to be in this mood. As I toweled off my hair, I walked back inside without looking over my shoulder. I hadn't seen her today, but that didn't mean she wasn't there. It just meant I hadn't noticed the curtains move or the coffee cup reflecting the light.

Mad Dog glanced back from where he stood at the counter. "Getting another cup of coffee. Want one?"

"In a bit. I'm going to shower first."

"Mindy said to tell you Merry Christmas." He leaned against the counter, acting all casual as if this wasn't the first time he'd mentioned her since that day by the woodpile.

"Thanks. Tell her I said the same."

"Too late. She already left. Probably while you were

working out." He pushed off the counter and walked toward the door.

I cut him off, blocking his exit. "She hasn't said a word to me about moving out."

"No one said anything about moving out. It's Christmas. She's going *somewhere* to celebrate with *someone*. I don't know the details. Even if I did, I wouldn't tell you because we don't talk about Mindy."

"Right." Curiosity was going to eat me alive before the holiday was over. "Does Ava know?"

"Don't worry. I told all the ladies not to talk to you about Mindy at all. About anything." He stepped around me. "I better get to it. You have Christmas plans? Are the restaurant hours changing for the holiday?"

"Yeah. Staff needs to celebrate. We'll be closed Christmas Eve, and Christmas dinner will be by reservations only. And Stephanie and I will get together at some point."

"You know you and your sister are welcome to join us at the ranch for Christmas Eve and/or Christmas morning. It's an open invitation."

"Thanks." Without my parents around, it was easier to bury myself in work, but that wasn't fair to my employees and their families. "Go make sure my ranch is running. I'll catch you later."

It had become part of my routine to check for Mindy's blue car. Now that it wasn't there, my brain conjured up all sorts of questions. And none of my friends would answer them.

Maybe she was spending Christmas with someone special. It didn't make sense that a woman like her would be completely unattached. But whoever she was dating didn't have much sense. He hadn't been out to see her new place. He didn't come pick her up to take her out on dates.

I would've noticed if there had been a man hanging around.

Trying to focus my thoughts onto something more productive, I glanced over my reservation list for Christmas Day and tried to decide what to serve. I scribbled down a couple of my favorites, then added a sea bass to the menu.

My choices had nothing to do with Mindy.

CHAPTER 13

*D*riving to the coast gave me lots of time to think. That was never a good thing.

After a week of what was obvious avoidance from Jeffrey, I'd contacted a realty agent to ask about other rentals in the area. One minute, I was plastered to the man's back as he gave me a horseback ride to work and helped me get away from a bull. The next two weeks, he'd hurried inside the moment my door creaked open.

I'd learned two things from the agent. One—there were only a few other places available in the area, but none were as close to the venue. And two—all the places were way more expensive than what I was currently paying. Jeffrey had to know that. Why had he made the rent so cheap?

My first inclination had been to assume that because of his friendship with everyone on the ranch, he was taking pity on me. But the look in his eyes after he'd lectured Lilith about the bull episode was not a pitying look. Labeling it was too dangerous, but it was very obviously not pity. That look made it a bad idea to continue living next door to him, but it also convinced me to stay.

At least for now.

With continued avoidance, our proximity wouldn't be an issue, and I wouldn't feel in his debt if I returned his good deed with one of my own. And I knew just the thing.

Donna waved from outside the cabin as I parked in front. "Debra and Denise ran to the store. The husbands are out doing last-minute shopping." She wrapped me in a hug. "How are you? Good drive?"

"It wasn't too bad, and I'm good. This place looks awesome."

"Wait until you see inside. We came out here this summer, and I just knew it would be perfect. There are four bedrooms with a king in each room. So, if you'd brought someone special along, there would've been room."

I hated that Jeffrey's face popped into my head when she mentioned bringing someone along. How many people needed to tell me I wasn't his type before my brain got the memo? So far, only one person had said it, and it hadn't made a dent in my attraction. But my determination to resist his charms was still strong.

Reading the posts about him over and over hadn't cemented the idea of him being a heartbreaking flirt. It made me think he had changed. He came home late after working at the restaurant, but I never saw any women around the place.

I would've noticed.

Besides, his friends talked about what a good guy he was. I'd seen it for myself. He'd dropped everything and rushed to the venue when I'd called him.

It was easier to convince myself I wasn't his type than to hope for a spark.

"It's just me." I pushed open the door and followed her to my bedroom. It was the only bedroom on the main floor, which was nice. The love birds could enjoy the upstairs space.

She leaned on the doorframe as I set my bag on the bed. "We decorated. I think you'll like it."

"How fun! How's your stuff going? I saw that you have a new sponsor."

Donna beamed. Her blog had taken off in a wild way, but it was clear she loved it just as much as she had when it was only a side gig done for fun. Now it was her full-time job and earned her real money. "It's fantastic. Toby and I have been eating out a lot. I'm trying to narrow down my list for my Valentine's suggestion post. And I need to find a place to eat on Valentine's Day. My traffic that day is through the roof, and I'm hoping to spotlight a lesser-known place that's fabulous." She lived between Austin and San Antonio but traveled all over for the blog.

"I think I know just the place." I had details to iron out, like how to pull this off without Jeffrey knowing I played any part in it, but setting it up so Donna blogged about his restaurant was the best way to make up for my primitive comment. The one about his food, not about him.

She wiggled her eyebrows. "I'm intrigued. Tell me more."

"I haven't tasted the food because of, you know, the meat and gluten allergies, but I know it's good. Very good."

She pointed toward the living room. "There's cider warming on the stove. Let's grab a cup, and you can give me the lowdown on this place. Where is it?"

We rounded the corner into the living room. A twelve-foot tree was draped with lights and sparkly snowflake ornaments. Under it were impeccably wrapped presents.

"Donna, you outdid yourself. This place looks fantastic. Very festive." I accepted the mug and perched on a stool. "The restaurant is near where I work, and it caters a lot of the gatherings at the venue. People rave about the food. It's at a winery and is run by a guy called the Cowboy Chef." I left out all the parts about Jeffrey being my landlord and way too hot for a man over fifty.

"I'm there. Cowboy Chef were the magic words. Send me the name of the place, and I'll see about getting a reservation. I try to go without anyone knowing so it can be a surprise on Valentine's Day. Word has a way of getting out."

"Let me handle that for you. I think I have a way to get you a table. And no one will know who it's for." I sipped my hot drink. "I know people."

"Perfect. Just send me the details once it's settled so I can book a room nearby."

"You are welcome to stay at my place, but since it's Valentine's, I understand if you'd rather make other arrangements."

"I appreciate the offer, but I'm wanting a cozy and romantic cabin for our mini getaway. And for my post about places to stay." She lifted her shoulders and sighed as they dropped. "We've been married almost two years, and I'm more in love now than when he proposed. I'd given up on the idea of finding someone, then boom."

Nodding, I took another sip. I knew about giving up. But I didn't expect the boom.

The door swung open, and Denise squealed. "I can't believe we made this happen. Christmas will be awesome."

Debra hefted grocery bags onto the table. "It will be. And they are predicting warm weather, so we can stroll on the beach and not be cold."

Celebrating with friends beat the solo Christmas I'd survived last year. I lifted my mug. "To y'all and our fantabulous Christmas."

Denise and Debra quickly filled mugs and joined Donna and me in the toast. "To us. And lifelong friends."

Donna's husband chuckled as he stepped inside. "Y'all drinking already? It's not even two."

"We haven't spiked the cider yet." Denise pointed at a stash of bottles on the counter. "But we will later."

Her husband walked up beside her and nuzzled her neck. "And then things will get interesting."

Being the odd one out wasn't much fun, but it was better than being lonely.

WHILE THE COUPLES finished decorating their gingerbread houses, I slipped into the bedroom and dialed Lilith's number. I'd expected to leave a message, but she answered after the second ring.

"Mindy? How are you?"

"I'm great. Some friends and I are celebrating at the coast." I sat on the edge of the bed. "I just called to ask a favor."

"Sure thing. What do you need?"

I swallowed, hoping she wouldn't detect too much emotion in my voice. "Do you know if there's any possibility I could get a table at Jeffrey's restaurant on Valentine's Day? But the thing is, I don't want him to know it's me reserving it."

"Let me see what I can do. I'll be in touch." She clicked her tongue. "I am curious. Is there someone special you haven't mentioned?"

Dang it. There was Jeffrey's smiling face again. If all my friends could stop using the phrase *someone special*, this phenomenon might stop. "Nothing like that. But please don't mention my name."

"All right. Have a merry Christmas."

"Same to you." I ended the call, knowing I'd have to wait several days for an answer. I didn't like waiting.

But ten minutes later, my phone buzzed.

Lilith: Table for two reserved for Valentine's. Jeffrey will think Beau and I are planning to have a romantic dinner that night. Your name isn't associated with the reservation. And I won't mention it to anyone else either.

Me: Thank you so much.

Now I had to wait until Valentine's Day. I doubted much would change between now and then, and Jeffrey would never guess I'd suggested his place to receive some online love.

CHAPTER 14

JEFFREY

*E*very noise pulled me to the window, curious if Mindy's blue car had returned. It was Christmas Day, so she was likely still with the person lucky enough to be enjoying her company during the holiday. After a quick glance, I had no explanation for the noise, so I resumed setting the table.

The handmade mesquite table looked best without a covering, so I opted for two placemats. Stephanie and I always sat at one end across from each other when we had a holiday meal together.

The house was decorated enough that someone walking in would know it was Christmas, but not so much that I'd be spending hours putting everything away. I made sure the tree lights were on before sliding the rolls into the oven. My sister was rarely late, and in five minutes, I expected her to walk in the door. When she did, everything would be ready.

Three minutes later, I was at the window again. Stephanie climbed out of her SUV with a large gift bag in one hand. The holidays were different now. Before my parents died, we'd enjoyed the typical family Christmas. Then there were several years when Stephanie hosted, but that ended when her husband died. Now, I hosted. If left to Stephanie, Christmas would be treated like any other day of the week. This year was better than last, so maybe she'd turned a corner in dealing with her grief.

She set the bag under the tree, then walked into the dining room. "It smells amazing in here. Thanks for cooking."

I hugged her. "Happy to do it. Can I get you a drink? I have sweet tea, Dr Pepper, and water."

"Dr Pepper. And if you have any vanilla, I'd love a little of that mixed in." She knew I kept a stash of syrups for specialty drinks.

"Coming right up. Have a seat."

Once I was back at the table, we served ourselves food, and she updated me on the happenings at the winery. She'd started it with her husband and had continued to build the business after his death. That place was what had kept her from being pulled under by her grief.

A clank outside caught my attention, but if I left the table to look outside, my sister would start asking questions I didn't want to answer. For lots of reasons. But mainly because I didn't have good answers. I couldn't explain why I cared so much about where Mindy was spending her holiday or more importantly with whom she was spending her holiday.

"Do you have a lot of reservations for tomorrow?"

Nodding, I forced myself not to look over my shoulder when another noise sounded. "More than I expected."

"That's good, right? Keep this up, and you'll be able to expand." She sipped her drink. "How's it going with your tenant?"

"What?" I stabbed a bite of turkey.

She pushed her plate out of the way and folded her arms,

eyeing me. "Spill it. You've said absolutely nothing about her. You jump every time there is a noise outside, and now you are trying to avoid a very simple question. What's going on with you and that woman?"

"Her name is Mindy, and there's nothing going on."

"Why not?" As a little sister, Stephanie had mastered the teasing smile. It used to annoy me, but now I liked seeing any of her smiles, teasing or otherwise.

I pushed my plate out of the way and leaned back. "I'm done dating women twenty years younger than me." There were days when the loneliness made it hard to hold to my resolve, but my stubborn streak helped in my weaker moments.

"How old is she?"

"Don't know. That's not something I typically ask women." I stood and stretched. "Coffee?"

"Yes, but we aren't done with this conversation."

I made sure she saw me roll my eyes before I stepped away from the table.

Stalling didn't work well because she followed me into the kitchen. "You want to meet someone, don't you?"

"Ideally, yes."

"If you were going to write up a personal ad, what would it say?" She stirred cream and sugar into her mug of coffee.

"I'm not interested in taking out a personal ad."

"That's not what I said. I asked what it would say. What do you want?"

What I wanted now was different than what I wanted years ago. Before, I wanted someone pretty who stroked my ego. That wasn't what I wanted now. I pictured Mindy, trying to articulate what precisely I found so attractive about her.

"Someone closer to my age. I mean, she could be in her forties."

"Besides age."

"I'm not sure what the point of this exercise is." We didn't have deep heart-to-heart conversations often, and this one made me especially uncomfortable.

"Tell me about your new tenant."

"She's tall, blonde, intelligent. She called me primitive and has obviously heard about my past escapades. Also, she's a pescatarian."

"I can't wait to meet her." Stephanie reached into her purse and slapped a deck of cards onto the table. "Want to open gifts now or later?"

"Now. Cards can wait."

She carried her coffee into the living room and dropped onto the sofa.

"Don't get too comfortable. Your gift is outside." I nodded toward the back door.

I'd put a lot of thought into what to get my sister, but I hadn't attempted to wrap it.

She hurried out to the back porch and stopped. If I hadn't been expecting that reaction, I might've crashed into her back. Lips pinched together, she spun around to face me. "Those are gorgeous."

"The wood is from here on the ranch, and I found a guy to make the benches. I thought they'd go well on that big front porch at your new house."

"They'll be perfect. Thank you."

"I'll load them in the truck and take them to your house later." I stuffed my hands in my pockets.

"They look like the stuff grandpa made, but that was the point, wasn't it?"

"I had the guy come see the pieces grandpa made."

Eyes wide, Stephanie looked at me, then at Mindy's house. "What did you do with the furniture in the house? Please tell me you didn't get rid of it."

"Seriously? Of course I didn't get rid of it. Mindy loved it, so I left it in the house."

"Good. Okay, now it's your turn. Let's go in so you can open yours. Then I'll beat you at cards."

"Beat me? I let you win."

"Whatever." She returned to her spot on the sofa and pointed at the only gift under the tree. "Open it."

I pulled the tissue out of the bag and smiled at the rose bushes. As I read the tag, my fingers itched to dig in the garden and add these to the array of roses already there. "I haven't worked out there in weeks, and I need to. This is perfect."

"They are like the ones Mom loved so much, but they're a pale apricot color."

"Belinda's Blush. I've read about them. Thank you."

Because we were both single and able to get the things we wanted, gift-giving was sometimes a challenge. We couldn't give each other what we wanted most, so we gave gifts with a memory attached, and I loved it.

A car door slammed, and Stephanie laughed. "You should go see if it's the tenant you aren't interested in."

"Maybe it's Mad Dog. Sometimes Ava sends him over with goodies." My stomach sank when I spotted Mindy's blue car. Had she planned to return home on Christmas day or had something gone wrong?

CHAPTER 15

*W*hy had I checked my email? It could've waited until I returned home tomorrow, but I wasn't good at forgetting about work. Reading that the caterer wouldn't be able to cover the New Year's Eve party because of a family emergency had zapped my festive mood, and as soon as we'd cleaned up after the meal, I'd hit the road.

What were the chances Jeffrey had room in his calendar for a catering job that day? Not good. In my short time at the venue, I'd learned he was usually booked out weeks in advance. But I had to at least ask.

But there was an SUV I hadn't seen before parked in front of his place, and since it was Christmas, it wasn't a stretch to assume he had company. I'd ask later.

The key didn't want to slide into the lock on my back door. Probably because I was so jumpy my hands weren't steady. The party was a big deal, and I needed to make sure it went smoothly. If I could have the food issues ironed out soon, then I could just fill Lilith in on the changes.

I finally won the battle with the lock, and the door swung open. A streak of gray brushed past my leg. If Sir Lancelot did his business in the herb garden, Jeffrey would never say yes to catering the party.

My bag and purse got dumped by the door, and I took off after my little deviant. Hopefully, no one was peeking out a window to witness the crazy cat chase.

"Sir." I scanned the front of Jeffrey's house, but my cat was nowhere to be seen. I'd have to check around back.

As I rounded the corner, the back door opened. "Hi! I'm Stephanie. You must be Mindy."

Now was not when I wanted to meet Jeffrey's newest squeeze.

"Hi. Yes. I'm looking for my cat. He rushed out the door, which he's never done before." I focused my attention on the small patch of tilled earth with only a few plants in it.

"Gray? I think I saw him racing toward the barn. I'll help you look." She walked around the far side of the house.

I glanced at the open door. Jeffrey leaned against the frame and gave a small nod. After a wave, I hurried to catch up with the woman. She was short and curvy, but older than I would've expected for Jeffrey. She was probably my age.

Maybe he had changed and was now dating women closer to his own age.

I crossed a grassy area and breathed a sigh of relief. Stephanie was holding Sir Lancelot.

"Thank you. I'm glad you found him." I extended my arms to take my poorly behaved feline. "So sorry to interrupt your holiday gathering."

"No bother. You should join us. Jeffrey and I were just about to play cards, and between you and me, I get tired of beating him all the time." She laughed and her dark hair danced on her shoulders.

"Oh, no. I don't want to impose. Merry Christmas." It was a short walk back to the house, and I hoped to make it without having her ask again. This day had already taken a turn for the worse. I didn't need to spend the rest of it with Jeffrey and his girlfriend.

"Please. Since you live here, I'd like to get to know you better." She glanced from me to Jeffrey.

Of course she would. She probably wanted to make sure I wasn't scheming to cut in on her territory. With a deep breath, I reminded myself that I wasn't his type, then turned around and smiled. "Okay. Let me put the cat away. Then I'll be over."

"Perfect. And it's nice to meet you, Mindy."

"Nice to meet you too." I rushed back to the house, scolding Sir as I went. "Thanks for nothing. I wasn't gone that long, and you had plenty of food and water. Did you spend the whole time plotting your great escape?"

The cat flicked his tail after I set him down and sauntered over to his food bowl. I added a bit to cover the dime-sized gap that made the bottom of the bowl visible.

"Now that you aren't starving, please be good. I'll be back." I closed the door without locking it and walked across the driveway.

Jeffrey opened his door before I had a chance to knock, then stepped aside for me to enter. "Merry Christmas. Can I get you a cup of coffee?"

"Please."

"Head on into the dining room. Stephanie's in there." He pointed off to the right.

Plates full of cookies were laid out on the table, and Stephanie tapped the chair at the end of the table. "Sit here. Jeffrey's getting coffee for you. Help yourself to dessert. Everything he makes is fabulous."

While the sweets all looked to die for, I didn't feel like asking about ingredients. Chances were high I couldn't eat them, so I shook my head. "No thanks. They look great though."

She picked up a cookie and took a bite. "How did you meet Jeffrey?"

I debated between simply answering her question and launching into assurances that I wasn't aiming to get Jeffrey's attention. I decided to just answer the question because if I let my mouth run, I'd end up telling her about the horseback ride and how he'd saved me from the bull, and that hug afterward when I couldn't stop shaking. Talking about those things with his girlfriend wouldn't end well. And ruining his Christmas wasn't a good way to make him inclined to help with the catering for the party. I didn't want to ruin his holiday whether it affected me or not.

"I work at the venue, and he caters many of the events there. The woman who owns the place—"

"Lilith?"

"Yes, she told me he had a place for rent."

"Interesting." She bit off another chunk of the cookie. "Do you like living here on the ranch?"

Jeffrey set a mug in front of me. "Stephanie, leave her alone. Let's play cards."

"What?" She lifted her eyebrows, feigning innocence, but there was no hint of jealousy on her face. Only tease.

He sat in the chair opposite Stephanie and dealt the cards. "I've let her win for forty-six years. It'll be fun to play to win tonight."

She laughed. "You wish. You're just bad at cards."

Forty-six years? Confusion must've shown on my face because Stephanie patted my hand.

A tender smile softened Jeffrey's strong masculine features. "She was about two when we started playing. Had no clue what she was supposed to do, but playing cards entertained her. And we were all happier when she won." He shuffled the deck. "And I've continued that goodwill all these years."

Stephanie rolled her eyes. "My brother is a great cook but horrible at cards."

"I'm pretty good at poker. Want to play that?" He dealt cards to the three of us.

The sibling banter was much more entertaining than watching Sir sleep.

"Well, maybe he won't lose tonight. I'm not great at cards myself." I picked up what he'd dealt me.

She chose another cookie off the plate. "Y'all have that in common."

I didn't need people telling me what I had in common with Jeffrey. Reminders that I wasn't his type were much better, given my current mindset. Seeing him as a doting brother did enough to stir my feelings.

Knowing I'd intruded on a family get-together seemed worse than crashing a date.

Two hours later, after I'd somehow won multiple hands, Stephanie stretched. "I should go. This has been fun, and we should definitely do it again."

Jeffrey picked up dishes as he stood. "I'll load the benches and be at your place in a bit."

That was my cue to scurry on home. I'd missed my chance to ask Jeffrey about catering when we were relaxed and having fun, but they were ready for the evening to be over.

Stephanie tapped my arm. "If you have time, you should come see the winery. Have you been there?"

"I've only been to the restaurant."

"Are you free now? You can ride with me." She pointed outside. "It's not far away, but you know that."

"Sure." I'd enjoyed the time playing cards and could

imagine being friends with Stephanie. "Let me just make sure Sir is behaving; then I'll be ready to go."

"Your cat's name is Sir?" She quirked an eyebrow.

"Sir Lancelot, but I shorten it to Sir."

Jeffrey leaned on the back of a chair. "His coloring is like a suit of armor."

No one had ever guessed the reason for his name, and my gaze snapped to Jeffrey to see if there was any hint of tease on his expression.

But he had the same look I'd seen after he'd lectured Lilith.

Stephanie cleared her throat. "I'll meet you out there when you're ready."

How long had I been staring at Jeffrey? "Right. I won't be long." I hurried back to the house.

Sir Lancelot was sound asleep in the middle of my bed, so I locked the door and walked over to Stephanie's blue SUV.

She started the engine as I climbed into the passenger seat. "This will be so fun. Jeffrey can drive you home later."

Now I wasn't sure if she wanted to show me the winery or if this was an elaborate ploy to have me spend time with her brother. She, of all people, should know I wasn't his type.

CHAPTER 16

JEFFREY

*W*hen I parked in front of Stephanie's, her SUV was there, but my sister and Mindy weren't anywhere in sight. I unloaded the benches and arranged them on the porch. Then I dropped onto one and waited.

The minutes ticked by as I waffled between being frustrated with my sister for trying to play matchmaker or being thankful that I'd get a few minutes alone with Mindy. Despite my feelings about her, I was glad Mindy and Stephanie had met. My sister had pulled away from people after being widowed, and tonight, there were glimpses of the old Stephanie, one who wasn't mired in grief.

That was another reason, beyond the age gap, to keep things friendly and professional with Mindy. That friendship was important, and I guessed that was true both ways. Showing any interest risked souring things, so I wouldn't.

Laughter echoed before they came into view, and a second later, the ladies walked around a stand of trees and down the path toward the house.

Stephanie's smile widened as she stepped onto the porch. "Those look great!" She hugged me, then hooked a thumb over her shoulder toward Mindy. "She came home early because the caterer canceled for the New Year's Eve party, and she's having to scramble to find someone else last minute. Will you handle it?"

Eyes wide, Mindy swallowed. "I don't want to impose. You are probably already booked. I'm sure I can find someone else."

"I'll do it." Not showing interest didn't mean I couldn't make her life a little easier.

"You aren't already scheduled for something?" She inched closer.

"The restaurant is closed New Year's Eve and New Year's Day, so I didn't book anything."

Mindy shook her head. "I don't want to—"

"I have a few employees who will be happy to work a few extra hours. It's not a big deal." I stuffed my hands in my pockets. "We can talk about the menu on the drive back."

Mindy turned and wrapped my sister in a hug. "Thank you. And I'll call you about getting together."

"Awesome." Stephanie pushed open her front door. "See y'all later."

I motioned for Mindy to walk to the truck. Then I walked around her to open the passenger door. She stayed quiet as she climbed in and buckled her seat belt.

Once we were rolling, I broke the silence. "Do you have the list of what the other caterer was going to provide?"

"I do. It's at the house."

"I know it's Christmas, but if you have time, we can go over it when we get back. I'll probably be able to make everything on the list."

"I'd feel better if we talked about it today, but I don't want to interfere with your holiday plans. And changes are fine. Whatever works for you."

"My holiday plans were to have Christmas dinner with my sister and lose at cards. That's all been covered."

She laughed, and something melted between us. Only a little. "I really appreciate this."

When she hated me, it was much easier not to show interest. This new dynamic would be harder to navigate.

"You're welcome. I planned to be at the party anyway."

"Did you make those benches? They're amazing."

"I only chopped down a few trees. I had someone else craft them. My talents are in the kitchen and do not extend to woodworking."

She turned and stared out the window. "Well, they're nice."

I parked, and she hopped out of the cab before I even had my door open.

"Let me grab the menu, and I'll be back in two minutes."

"Just come on in."

Three minutes later, the door opened, and Mindy called out, "Knock, knock."

"I'm in the kitchen."

She laid the menu on the table and sat with her hands folded, waiting while I filled two mugs with coffee.

"Here you go. Cream and sugar are on the table." I sat in the chair next to her. "Let's see what's on here."

I ran my finger down the list. "We could add popcorn shrimp for people like you who'd rather eat seafood."

"Sure. That's fine."

"Then you'd be able to eat something other than veggies."

Her shoulders tensed, and her lips pinched.

"But you don't eat fried shrimp, I'm guessing."

Shaking her head ever so slightly, she stared at the table a second before looking at me. "I'm celiac, so I can't have most fried foods."

"Which is why you only looked longingly at the cookies but never ate any."

"That's why. It's easier to skip eating things rather than explain the reasons I don't eat them."

I jumped up. "You like chocolate?"

"I love it. Why?"

"You'll see." I turned on the oven to preheat and pulled what I needed out of my cabinets and fridge.

She walked up to the counter. "You don't have to make anything for me. Really. That's not why I told you."

"Mindy, it's Christmas. I'm making a dessert you can eat. Now, back to the menu. Any other changes you'd like to make? Instead of popcorn shrimp, we could do shrimp cocktails. We can put them in clear plastic cups, and they'd be self-serve and easy cleanup."

"That sounds good. And the rest is fine. You don't have to worry about drinks." She leaned on the counter, watching me as I worked. "I really don't think your food is primitive."

"Only me then?" I kept my gaze on the stove as I melted chocolate and butter. "It might be a fair assessment."

"One I should've kept to myself."

"Truce?" I wiped my hand on a rag and held it out.

"Sure. But just to clarify, is this only for today—like the Christmas truce during World War I—or more long term?"

"I was thinking long term."

She clasped my hand and gave it a shake. "I like that idea."

I liked the idea a lot. At this rate, we might even work our way to friends, which meant we might spend more time together. This was going to cause a problem at some point, but for now, I chose to enjoy how things were.

I separated the eggs and added sugar to the yolks before turning on the mixer.

"What are you making?"

"A chocolate soufflé cake. There isn't any flour in it. Just butter, chocolate, eggs, and sugar. Oh, and a pinch of salt."

She sighed. "That sounds delectable."

"It'll take a bit, so maybe we'll play a few rounds of cards. And while it cools, I'll whisk up some fresh whipped cream."

She watched as I mixed the ingredients, then stepped out of the way as I slid the cake pans into the oven.

"When you're making the whipped cream, I'm happy to help with whatever."

"You can cut up the strawberries."

As I set the timer, she walked toward the dining room. "Having a truce doesn't mean I'm going to let you win at cards."

"Good to know. I won't lose on purpose."

Her grin made my insides do a dance. Thanks to an unpredictable cat and my meddling sister, I was enjoying a great Christmas.

And soon, Mindy would be indulging in dessert.

ON NEW YEAR'S EVE, I'd only caught glimpses of Mindy as she hurried around the venue. I'd gotten all the food set up, and in a short time, the venue would be bustling with people.

Lilith's New Year's Eve party was the talk of the town, and I expected there to be a packed house. But I'd made plenty of food, so there was no risk of people going home hungry.

After checking Chuck's pen, to be sure he'd been moved to the back pasture, I carried a small cooler into the office building. Mindy was leaning over her desk, and I allowed myself a short stare.

"Dinner." I set the bag on the desk.

She chewed the end of her pen as she stared at papers on the desk. "Thanks. You can leave it there."

I dropped into a chair and unzipped the top of the bag. "I brought you a steak and fried chicken. Sound good?"

Nodding, she didn't look up. "Yeah. I'll get to it in a bit."

"And the raccoon skewers are hot and ready for everyone. I was hoping to let Chuck hang out here in your office. All that fine with you?"

She blinked as she glanced up. "What did you say about chucking raccoons?"

I laughed. "Eat. I brought you a shrimp cocktail and a sandwich. The bread is gluten-free."

Mindy eased into her desk chair. "Thank you. I've only had coffee today, so this is really nice."

"I know you don't have much time, but take a few minutes to eat. Please."

"I will. I've been over this list a hundred times, but I want everything to be perfect."

"The place looks amazing. It'll be great."

After eating a piece of shrimp, she pulled the curtain aside and looked out the window. From her desk, she could see the parking lot and entrance to the venue. "The band should be here soon." She tasted the sandwich. "This is incredible. The bread . . ." She took another bite and sighed. "Did you make this bread?"

"I did. Glad you like it." I handed her a napkin and pointed to a spot of my special sauce on her lower lip. "I'm going to check the food again. Holler if you need me."

"Jeffrey."

Turning, I reminded myself that she likely wanted me to do something; it wasn't me she wanted. "Yes?"

"Have you eaten?"

"I ate a sandwich."

"Good because by midnight, you'd probably be hangry." She pulled a water bottle out of the cooler.

"We wouldn't want that." I strolled back to the big room to check on the buffets.

Being nice to Mindy was even more enjoyable than needling her and trying to get her to dislike me.

Way more enjoyable.

CHAPTER 17

*S*tanding near the back wall, I finally started to relax. There was an hour until midnight, and everyone seemed to be having a wonderful time. I'd heard so many comments about the amazing food, and people were already asking if we'd be hosting a party again next year.

Couples danced as the band played. Watching how each set of dancers moved as one captivated me. My gaze swept back and forth across the room. I told myself I was monitoring the party and checking for problems, but when I spotted Jeffrey, my scanning paused.

He stood at the edge of the dance floor with his arms crossed. His focus was on the dancers, and not on the short blonde walking toward him. She had to be half his age. Maybe even younger than that. My lip-reading skills weren't honed enough to make out what she said to him, but with her thumb hooked over her shoulder, pointing toward the dance floor, I could wager a guess.

Jeffrey shook his head. That was a bit of a surprise.

The air changed as someone eased up beside me. This was the awkward moment where I had to choose between turning to face the person, which meant committing myself to exchanging words, or acting like I hadn't noticed.

"I bet if you asked him to dance, he'd say yes." Tandy nudged my arm. "You should go ask him."

I chose not to respond to her suggestion, hoping she'd forget about it. "Hey, Tandy, are you having fun?"

She shrugged. "Meh. It's too cold for guys to be running around without shirts, but besides that, it isn't so bad." The crinkles near her eyes appeared like always when she teased.

I was learning to pick up on those details. "I'm so sorry everyone is fully clothed."

"I suppose I'll live. Are you going to ask him?"

Another woman was now talking to Jeffrey. "No. I need to make sure everything runs smoothly."

"Well, it looks to me like your caterer is trapped by some young'un who finds him dignified. You should rescue him."

"I don't think—"

"My dear, that's not true. Your biggest problem is that you do think. Way too much." She waved at Jeffrey and motioned him over. "I've seen the way y'all look at each other. Sparks like that should be fanned and fueled. Not starved of oxygen."

His gaze bounced between me and Tandy as he wove through the crowd.

Tandy waved to another man, one I'd seen at the venue before, and he headed our way. "Or, if you want Jeffrey to make the first move, give him a reason. Dallas is one of the only ranch hands who doesn't run from me. I don't ask him to pose without a shirt because he's quieter than all the rest. Anyway, he's a tad shorter than you, but he's a good dancer. Ask him."

I swallowed back my frustration and turned to face her. "If I want to dance—" Words stuck in my throat when a familiar cologne wafted around me.

And if I didn't know Jeffrey had walked up, Tandy's face gave it away.

"Hey." His deep voice made it easy to hear him even with the din of the crowd.

She grinned. "What were you saying about wanting to dance?"

Before anyone responded to Tandy, the band announced they were taking a break. The deejay took over. The Electric Slide started playing, and dancers lined up on the floor.

"I said I didn't want to dance because I was making sure everything ran smoothly. Besides, it wouldn't look very professional for me to be cutting a rug."

Jeffrey bumped my shoulder with his. "I'm not sure Lilith would agree. Look at her out there trying to teach Beau the dance steps."

"I'm glad she's enjoying herself. Anyway, line dancing really isn't my thing."

Tandy laughed. "You prefer being wrapped in a man's arms? I can't blame you for that."

Dallas hovered a few steps away, then walked up. "Did you need something, Miss Tandy?"

"I need you to dance with me when the band starts playing again."

He nodded. "Sure thing."

She patted his shoulder, then looped her arm around his. "Have you eaten? I want more food. It's so tasty."

They wandered off, leaving me standing beside Jeffrey. This wasn't a big deal. We were friends, but anytime we interacted, I worried he'd pick up on my attraction. Liking a guy who wasn't interested usually ended in embarrassment, whether in middle school or after forty. I was trying to beat the odds on that.

He crossed his arms and scanned the crowd.

If one of us didn't say something soon, it would be

awkward, so I opened my mouth and let words fall out. "Lots of people have said they loved the food. Thank you again for jumping in at the last minute to help me."

He nodded but kept his gaze on the dance floor. "No problem." After another second of silence, he shifted away from me. "I see Mad Dog over there. I'll catch you later."

"Sure. Okay." I leaned back against the wall, wishing I had the ability to cloak and become invisible.

It was hard enough watching a roomful of couples anticipating a New Year's kiss, but Jeffrey's obvious desperation to get away made it worse. He could be so kind, like when he'd shown up with dinner, and other times, he wouldn't even look at me and acted as if he were in a hurry to escape.

But sorting out his moodiness implied interest, and I was determined not to give into my attraction.

"Good night." I waved as the cleanup crew walked out. Checking the time would only exhaust me even more. People had partied until after two, and I expected the sun to be peeking over the horizon before I made it to my bed.

Walking through the venue, I made sure lights were off and doors were locked; then I headed to my office to get my purse and keys.

On the porch, a shadow moved, and I froze. Who else was still here?

"Hello?" I should've replaced that last bulb when the light flickered three days ago. Now that it was out, I couldn't make out who sat in the chair.

"Hey. Sorry. I must've dozed off." Jeffrey stretched as he stood. "Didn't want you out here all alone."

I tried to cover my shock, hoping the darkness hid the delight mixed in. "I thought you left hours ago."

"I drove Stephanie home, then came back. You were busy, so I found a spot to wait."

Being avoided was bad enough, but being treated like a little sister was even worse. "Out here, I'm not too worried. Chuck will protect me."

"Don't get mad. It's late, and I didn't want a woman out here alone."

I crossed my arms. "So did you stay out here with Lilith when she worked really late?"

He leaned on the wall next to me. "No, Beau did. Are we going to stand here arguing while you shiver, or are you going to get your things so I can ensure you make it home safely?"

His smug look was back, and it irritated me in the worst way. But as tired as I was, I didn't have it in me to argue with him. "I'll grab my things."

He opened the door and followed me inside. "You put on an incredible party tonight. Several people commented about how impressed they were. And I know Lilith appreciated it."

"Thanks." I handed him the cooler he'd brought in earlier. "This is yours. That sandwich was the best I've had. Do you sell that bread?" The answer probably wasn't yes, but it never hurt to ask.

"No, but I make it for friends. I have two loaves at the house for you." He switched off the light as I walked out of the room with my purse hooked over my shoulder. "Stephanie had a good time tonight. Thanks for inviting her."

"She's fun."

"She is, but she hasn't been going to parties since her husband died. I think your invitation tipped her decision. So, thanks."

I pulled my coat closed when the wind gusted. Sounds of laughter floated on the air. "Do you hear that?"

Jeffrey groaned. "People are still here. But where?"

We stepped off the porch, listening. This wind died down, and we started walking in the direction of the voices. Soon, we could make out the words.

"Look at his horns! You climb on, and I'll take a picture." The s was drawn out by the drunk slurring his words.

"Albert. That old goat finds all kinds of trouble when he's drunk. If I'd seen him earlier, I would've made sure someone escorted him home. I wonder who's with him." Jeffrey mumbled a few choice words, then grabbed my arm. "Did you eat the apple slices I put in the cooler?"

"Only a few. The rest are still in the bag. Why?"

"How do you feel about feeding a bull?" He tucked an arm around me. "I hate that no one else is here, but if I call and wait until someone gets here, these guys might not make it. No bull likes to be taunted. Come on."

I hurried to keep up with Jeffrey's pace. "Just tell me what to do."

Inside, every muscle twitched with fear, but I put on my brave face.

He pulled out his phone and used the flashlight to illuminate our path, and once we arrived at the back fence, he tapped my back. "Pull out the apple and wait here. I'm going to see if I can get those guys to leave voluntarily before anyone—man or beast—gets angry. If I manage to lure them away from Chuck, call the bull and offer him the apple. But *do not* go inside the fence. Got it?"

As if he had to tell me not to go into the field with the bull. I didn't care to live through that sort of fear again. Chuck seemed less scary after getting to know him a little, but the animal was still huge . . . and had horns. Long ones.

"Yes. Please be careful." I stared into the dark as two guys made their way closer to Chuck, who didn't seem all that irritated yet. Keeping my gaze focused on them, I slipped my phone out of my pocket and held it up so I could dial while still keeping Chuck in sight. Given the way these guys were three sheets to the wind, we'd need someone from the sheriff's department.

The dispatcher answered, and I sucked in a deep breath before spewing the problem at her. "So please send someone out to the venue. We are out at the back pasture. They can drive around the main building to get here."

"I'll get someone en route."

"Thanks." I ended the call and held my breath as Jeffrey strode closer to the guys. "Hey there, Albert! What are y'all up to out here?"

"This is our bull. Go find your own." Albert—who was clearly an angry drunk—stomped toward Jeffrey.

My stomach soured. This wasn't going to end well.

"Yeah!" The other guy, who was younger, stumbled after Albert.

Because of all the shouting, Chuck now looked irritated.

I didn't wait for the second guy to walk away from the bull. I yanked the apple slices out of the bag. "Hiya, Chuck. Want some apples?"

His head unhurriedly swung toward the fence.

"Come on, Chuck. I have a treat for you." I tried to hide the fear in my voice.

"You got something for me too?" The other drunk guy started toward the fence.

Now I had a bull and a fool walking this way.

Chuck continued his measured walk to the fence, and the drunk tumbled, then picked himself up off the ground. The possibility of him being trampled equaled that of being gored. Neither would be good for business.

The drunk made it to the fence first and started to climb over. At least one of the guys would be away from the bull, but I wasn't sure how I was going to keep him away from me because the way he was looking at me, the something he wanted was not apple.

As the guy flipped over the fence, yelling because it was made of barbed wire, Jeffrey called out, "Get away from her."

Snagged on the fence, the drunk grumbled to himself and ignored Jeffrey.

But Jeffrey's yelling had gotten Chuck's attention. The bull changed direction and trotted to where Albert and Jeffrey were engaged in a standoff. Albert was yelling, but the words were unintelligible, which made everything worse.

I ran for the gate. Chuck's head lowered, and he looked very displeased with all the company. "Come get the apple, Chuck. Look here." It took longer than normal to unlatch the gate. "Over here!" I jumped up and down and waved my arms.

"Mindy, what are you doing?" Jeffrey ducked as Albert threw a sloppy right hook.

With one drunk snagged on the fence and Jeffrey fighting the other, that left me to keep the bull from charging anyone. I prayed this beast really liked apple.

With my hand out, I inched closer to the massive creature, speaking as sweetly as I could. "Here you go. You like apple, don't you? I'm sorry these dimwits bothered you."

He stopped moving toward Jeffrey but didn't turn.

"Don't bother them. Walk this way." I held the apple as far out in front of me as my arms allowed. I'd never been more thankful for my long arms.

In slow motion, like something out of a cartoon, Chuck changed directions and made his way toward me.

I held my breath but didn't close my eyes.

"Mindy Lawrence, get out of this pasture!" Jeffrey sounded angrier than I'd ever heard him.

But I ignored him and sucked in a breath as Chuck nibbled the apple. After he ate one piece, I pulled another out of the bag. My plan to keep the bull away from Jeffrey would work great until I ran out of apple slices. There were only four left. I must've eaten more than I thought.

While I was trying to think of a plan B, bright lights swept the field and illuminated Chuck. He looked pretty cute eating out of my hand.

Car doors and voices sounded behind me, but I didn't dare look away. As Chuck munched the last bit of apple, I backed up ever so carefully, praying I lived long enough to make it to the fence.

A hand touched my back. "Stay behind me." Jeffrey did the same thing he'd done before and stepped in front of me. And just like last time, I plastered myself to his back as he grabbed my hand.

I held my questions until the gate closed. "Where are the guys?"

Jeffrey turned and wiped blood off his lip. "Deputy loaded them into the back of his car. He'll need to talk to you about what happened."

Overwhelmed and fighting tears, I wrapped my arms around his neck. "You got hurt. I'm so sorry."

"I'll be fine, but don't *ever* pull a stunt like that again. Didn't you hear me?"

"Every word, but he was getting irritated with the yelling and fighting, and I wasn't going to let him hurt you." At some point, I needed to let go of Jeffrey, but that was easier said than done.

His arms tightened around me, but a second later, he stepped back. "Go talk to the deputy. Then I'll take you home."

I nodded. Even though it was only a mile to his place, I didn't trust myself to drive, so I wouldn't argue with him.

Tightening my grip on his hand, I stopped him from walking away. "I'm really glad you waited for me."

"Yeah." He stuffed his hands in his pockets and strode toward the deputy.

After hugging him like that, he probably knew exactly how I felt, and the way he pushed me away left little doubt about his feelings. Or the lack there of.

At least my embarrassment had only been witnessed by a bull. The deputies were too busy trying to cram drunks into the back of the cruisers.

CHAPTER 18

JEFFREY

*D*riving Mindy home had meant that I'd have to take her to get her car today, but since she'd been shaking when she hugged me, driving her was the safer option.

As I knocked on her door, I renewed my resolve to hide my attraction. Before I'd reformed, if a woman had shown interest, I played along. Sometimes, there hadn't been attraction, but my ego liked the attention. With Mindy, there was enormous amounts of attraction. That was what made it so hard to be around her.

And after what she'd done last night, I needed to keep my distance. This wasn't just attraction anymore. I cared for her. Deeply.

It had been hard enough seeing her in the pasture with Chuck when he was obviously irritated by the drunks, but then she'd hugged me. I wouldn't flatter myself to think she was interested; she'd just been happy I hadn't gotten hurt.

But that didn't stop me from thinking about her. A lot.

She pulled open the door. "Give me half a sec."

Her blue turtleneck made her eyes sparkle, and there was a hint of expectation in her smile.

"Sure. And I brought that bread over."

"Just set it on the counter. And watch out for Sir. He's been trying to escape lately." She disappeared around the corner.

I set the bread down and scooped up the cat when he ran toward the door. "Morning. Where do you think you're going? She doesn't want you to go outside." When I scratched him behind the ears, he purred. "Like that, do you?"

Footsteps sounded, and I glanced up. The look on Mindy's face made two things perfectly clear. She was interested, and cuddling her cat was earning me points I didn't want.

After quickly putting the cat on the floor, I reached for the door. "Ready?"

"Yes. Thank you for taking me over. Did you get much sleep last night?"

"Enough." I'd be dead on my feet by tonight, but I'd survive. There was more concern about whether I'd get her dropped off before saying something I'd regret.

I opened the truck door, and she climbed into the passenger seat.

One mile. I could make it one mile.

She shifted so that she faced me. "The sheriff left a message. They kept the guys overnight so they could sober up. He didn't want them prowling around any other pastures and meeting bulls who weren't as nice as Chuck."

"Beer makes some people stupid." I turned into the venue and parked beside her car. "Have a good day."

"Thanks for the ride. I'll see you later." She climbed out and waved before walking into the office building.

If I could manage it, she wouldn't see me later. But I had

to make it look like we were just missing each other because I didn't want to hurt her.

TWO WEEKS PASSED, and I'd successfully avoided Mindy and hated every minute of it.

After checking the weather again, hoping that predictions had changed, I strode out to the barn.

As I stepped inside, Mad Dog rubbed his face. He'd been working long hours the last three days, prepping the ranch for the coming storm. "Did you get the extra couch arranged in the den?" The crinkles near his eyes guaranteed more ribbing was coming my way.

"The weather is unpredictable. If we lose power, her place is going to get cold quickly."

"And you want her in your . . ." He grinned. "I think you just want *her*."

"We've already discussed this. Of all people, I thought you'd support me and encourage my good behavior."

Mad Dog shrugged. "I've never seen you spend so much time thinking about someone you are determined not to date. I'm still getting used to the version of Jeffrey who's determined not to date."

"She deserves someone closer to her age."

"Or maybe you shouldn't assume what she wants or needs and *talk to her*." He cocked his head, giving me a look only dads could perfect.

"What do you need me to do? I closed the restaurant tonight. We don't need a bunch of people out here on our roads if they're right about what's coming." The change of subject would surely make it clear I was finished with the previous conversation.

"I think we're okay. Troughs are full. Spigots are dripping.

There's extra feed ready. And all exposed pipes on the well house and barn are covered. If the temps drop below freezing, I'll need to come out and break up ice, give the cows extra feed."

Mentally, I took inventory of what we had stacked in the barn. "Don't drive over unless I call you. How are things at Stargazer Springs?"

"Clint seems a bit stressed, but I think things are covered. It's been a long time since we've had an extended freeze in this area."

"I'm still hoping the forecast is wrong." I nodded toward the door. "Head on home. I'll call if I need anything."

Mad Dog tipped his hat and walked out of the barn. I followed and made sure the door was closed. If the weatherman was right, we were in for a cold week.

He waved as he drove toward the gate, and I headed back to the house. When it was frigid enough to snow, I skipped swimming. Besides, swimming made me think of Mindy.

Her car was parked in front of the house. After not seeing her for two weeks, I needed to make sure she was prepared for the coming weather. This wouldn't be awkward at all.

I dragged my boots across the doormat before knocking. When the door opened, surprise registered on her face. Then her surprise gave way to hurt for a second before her features solidified into something unreadable.

"Everything okay?" She kept the door partway closed and didn't invite me in.

Even though I felt like a heel, talking to her was imperative, and it was way too cold to stand outside and talk. "Mind if I come in?"

She shrugged and stepped back, letting the door swing open.

"Mindy, I'm sorry I haven't been around much. I—"

Her head wagged back and forth. "Please don't make

excuses. I get it, and it's fine. I'm sorry I made you uncomfortable. Now, what do you need?"

"Forecast is predicting frigid temps and possibly snow. More than a dusting. I wanted to be sure you had faucets dripping and plenty of food."

Her jaw set, she nodded. "I'm good. I've been keeping up with the weather updates."

The chill in here matched the temps outside. "You know where to find me if you need anything."

"Okay."

I turned away from her and grabbed the door handle. "You didn't do anything wrong, Mindy. I don't want you to think that."

"Okay."

I hated that word. She used it as a spear, wounding me a little more every time she used it.

Two okays in a row were painful enough; I opted not to go for three, so I slipped out and walked back to my house. She was hurt and angry. Figuring out how to solve the problem would take some creativity . . . or maybe just an honest conversation.

When I reached my door, I glanced at her house. The curtains moved a bit, making it obvious that she'd watched me walk away.

After what she'd read about me, telling her she was too young for me would sound like I was making excuses, which would only hurt her more. Just as soon as I figured out what to say, I'd have that conversation with her.

Snow flurries landed on my sleeve as I grabbed the doorknob. It would be a cold night.

CHAPTER 19

*W*hen I'd read that snow was predicted, I'd expected maybe an inch, two at most. But there was nearly a foot on the ground, and it was still snowing. Moonlight reflected off the snow, blanketing the ranch in a strange glow.

But staring out the window made me feel cold, so I curled up on the sofa and sipped my hot tea. I read a romance I'd had in my TBR pile for months and checked weather updates between chapters.

The lights flickered, and I jumped up once they were back on. Candles would be handy if I were plunged into darkness longer than a few moments. All I had to do was remember where I'd stored my candles. I wandered through the house, checking closets and cabinets. I finally found them in the small cabinet above the stove. Why had I put them there? I'd probably been distracted by my neighbor's swim time and hadn't been thinking clearly.

I arranged the candles on the coffee table with the torch lighter beside them and went back to reading. Before finishing a paragraph, darkness engulfed me. This time, there was no flicker. I felt around the table for the lighter, then lit the three candles.

If the power were off all night, I'd need multiple blankets or I'd wake up with icicles on my toes.

Reading by candlelight left a lot to be desired. So, with Sir snuggled on my chest and three blankets draped over us, I closed my eyes.

After lying there a while, I must've fallen asleep because I jumped when someone—I had a fairly good guess who—banged on the door. It startled Sir, and his claws dug into me.

I yanked his mini deadly weapons off my shirt and hurried to the door with a candle in my hand. "Coming." It was too cold to talk with the door open, so I motioned for Jeffrey to come inside.

"Come on. You can stay at my house until we have power again. I have a fireplace and a small generator. You'll freeze if you stay here." He glanced toward the living room. "And I'll get Sir. I bet he hates this."

If it weren't so cold in my house, I'd have sent Jeffrey home alone. But it was extremely cold, and the dark somehow made it feel colder.

I nodded. "Let me throw a few things in a bag."

"Thank goodness. I thought you'd argue with me."

"I'm too cold to argue."

"Well, that's one good thing about this blasted storm." He unzipped his coat. "Once I get the cat to my house, I'll come back for your stuff."

"What about all my food?"

"We'll either move stuff to my fridge or store it outside." He rubbed my shoulder and even through my multiple layers, I could feel the heat of his hand. "Wait inside until I get back."

"Just come back in. I won't be long."

I walked toward the hall but peeked around the corner in time to see Jeffrey nestle Sir Lancelot inside the coat. Now I was jealous of my cat. And not just because he was warm now that he was tucked up against that muscular chest. I wasn't jealous of the warmth; I was jealous of his being cuddled against Jeffrey.

Gah. I needed to stop thinking about muscles and pack enough for an overnight stay. Surely, the lights would be on by morning. I wasn't sure how long I'd last at Jeffrey's with my sanity intact.

As I tucked cat food and the bowls into a bag, Jeffrey walked into the kitchen. "Where's the litter? I'll carry that over."

"I scooped it a while ago, but I can't guarantee he hasn't used it. You don't have to get it. I can do that."

"It's fine. Just tell me where."

"The hall bathroom." I went back to packing up food for kitty and for me.

When he came around the corner, I opened the door for him. "I'll be over in just a minute."

"Be careful. I salted the driveway so follow my path because it's really slick and easy to fall on the ice. And I'm not sure how we'd get out of here with all this going on. The roads are probably horrible because it drizzled and snowed before the temps dropped below freezing."

"So there's ice everywhere. I'll be careful."

He cautiously made his way across the driveway, and I grabbed my bags and followed, making sure I stepped in his tracks. Landing on my butt right now would only make this night more awkward. Because no matter how much it hurt, I was not taking muscle relaxers.

Inside, there wasn't a fire blazing in the living room like I'd expected. I'd come thinking his place would be warmer.

"You stay in there, and I'll find you a treat. Sound good?"

Jeffrey was talking to Sir like I did, treating the cat as if he might answer back.

Following the sound of Jeffrey's voice, I walked around the living room and into the kitchen. "There you are. You aren't using the fireplace?"

"That area is wide open. There is a second fireplace in the den, so I set up camp in there. I hope that's okay."

"Yeah. Sure. Where should I put my things?"

Jeffrey rubbed the back of his neck as he walked out of the kitchen to a part of the house I hadn't yet seen. "You can put it in this room, but I figured we'd sleep in the den. It'll be warmer because there is a fireplace in an enclosed space. And the den is the room that has power. The generator provides limited power to the den and kitchen."

I stared at him while replaying his words in my head. Had I heard him correctly?

"Mindy, if you're uncomfortable with sleeping in the same room, I'll let you have the den."

"I'm not going to make you sleep in the cold and dark. I'm not cruel. Sleeping in the same room is fine."

"Once you're settled, I need to run and check on the animals. Temps are dropping lower than originally predicted." He backed against the wall and waited for me to walk around him.

With him like that, I didn't brush against his chest as I passed him. Too bad.

Inside the den, I dropped my bag near the wall. "You can't go out in this."

"I have to, but I shouldn't be longer than an hour or two." He zipped his coat up and again tapped the doorframe. "Help yourself to whatever you find in the kitchen. When I get back, we'll deal with the rest of your food."

"What should I do if you don't come back?"

He stepped closer to me. "I can tell you what you shouldn't do."

"What?" I crossed my arms, having a pretty good idea of what was coming.

"Do *not* come after me. Do *not* walk outside. Do *not* launch a one-woman rescue mission."

"That was a lot of *do nots*."

His eyebrows lifted. "I want you to understand me. Was it clear enough?"

"Yes."

"Promise me."

I shook my head. "I won't make that promise. If you're still gone in two hours, I'm not going to stay here, wondering where you are."

He sighed. "I'll just have to be back before you decide to ignore me."

"Yep." I kept my arms folded so I wouldn't hug him. "Please be careful."

He set a cowboy hat on his head before walking outside.

I'd never seen him in one before, and now my heart was thumping like a twitterpated rabbit. Dang that man.

Before he was out of sight, I ran outside. "Wait."

He tipped his head back, clearly frustrated I hadn't made it a full minute before doing what he'd told me not to do. "What?"

"Give me a sec to get my boots on. I'm going with you." I retraced the trail of footsteps back to my place, ignoring the look Jeffrey was giving me.

"And you're going to help take care of cattle because you have so much experience with them?"

"Chuck and I have become pretty good friends." I hurried inside, and with the help of my phone's flashlight, I searched my closet. Somewhere in here, I had waterproof hiking boots that I'd worn twice. But they'd be handy to have on tonight. Nothing was worse than wet socks.

I hurried, but if Jeffrey left without me—which was a distinct possibility—I'd just go to the barn and hope I caught him. But getting outside before he left would be preferable. I leaned my phone so I could see enough to tie the boots.

Footsteps thudded in the kitchen, and I smiled. "Almost done. Thank you for waiting."

"I only waited because you'd ignore me and wander around the ranch until you found me or froze to death."

I stepped into the kitchen and nodded. "That was my plan. Except the freezing-to-death part. I can't sit inside while you are outside. I'd rather help you."

His mouth opened, then snapped shut. "You can stop shining that light at my face. You're going to blind me."

"Sorry." I turned the light off, then rushed out the door. "We should hurry. It's getting colder."

"Brilliant advice." His hand brushed mine, and he stopped. "Where are your gloves?"

"I couldn't find them." I shoved my hands into my coat pockets. "I'll be fine."

Shaking his head, he opened the passenger door of the truck. "Hop in."

When I'd volunteered my help, I'd expected to walk, so riding in the truck was a pleasant surprise.

But even in the cab, it was frigid. It'd been much warmer under the pile of blankets in my cold house and even warmer in his house, but I wouldn't trade that for going with Jeffrey. He'd made it clear he wasn't interested, and I was behaving like a yapper dog, trying to get his attention, but right now, I didn't care. I wasn't letting him go out in this alone.

Shivering as he slid in behind the wheel, I said, "The snow finally stopped."

"Yep." He drove toward the barn.

"Are we riding horses?" That hadn't been a factor in my decision because the thought hadn't occurred to me. The only time I'd ever been on a horse was with Jeffrey, and getting cozy in the saddle didn't sound like such a horrible idea right now.

That maddening smirk was barely visible in the moonlight. "Why? You itching to ride horseback with me again?"

"Of course not." In the dark, he probably couldn't tell I was lying through my teeth.

"Wait here." He parked and walked around the corner of the barn.

An engine rumbled to life, so when he walked back, I was surprised. "What's that noise?"

"Generator." He held out his hand. "Be very careful where you step. I don't want you to fall."

Gripping his hand like my hip depended on it, I slid out of the truck. With all the grace of a baby giraffe on roller skates, I slipped on ice as soon as my foot met the ground. My feet slid in opposite directions, but strong arms wrapped around me, keeping me from landing on my butt.

Focusing on breathing in and out, I stayed pinned to his chest.

"Mindy." His voice was gravelly and deep.

I lifted my gaze to meet his. "Yeah?"

"I just told you not to fall."

"How am I supposed to avoid ice I can't see?"

"By staying in the house." He ran a gloved hand down my back and tugged me closer. "But you're out here now."

"Sorry."

"I'd just hate for you to have to take those pills." He winked, then let go of me and opened the barn. He flipped a switch, and a light came on.

The light distracted me from the comment about my pills,

but I stopped myself before asking how he'd worked that magic because I remembered the generator.

"I'll load hay and feed into the truck; then we'll go."

"Do you have the generator so you can run a heater for the horses?"

"They're fine in here without one for now. But it's cold enough I wouldn't take them outside. The generator is mainly for my well pump. No electricity. No water. Unless I get out here and use the hand pump, which I'd rather avoid."

"What about the cows? What happens to them?"

"I need to make sure they have plenty of food and water. If it stays below freezing too long, the troughs freeze over, and I'll have to break the ice. It hasn't been below freezing long enough for that yet, but I want to make sure the troughs are full, that no pipes have broken, and that everything seems okay. I'll also throw out a bit of extra hay and feed."

I rubbed my hands together. "Mad Dog said you grew up out here."

"I did. And this isn't the first time it's been this cold, but it's been a while." He yanked off his gloves. "Wear these until we get out there. I'll need them when I'm working, but it'll give your hands time to warm up."

"No. I can't take your gloves."

Leaning in close, he smiled, and a delightful shiver ran down my spine. "You aren't the only stubborn one. Take them."

His gloves were still toasty from his body heat. I was, too, but for an entirely different reason. This felt a little like flirting.

I'd remind myself that he didn't like me when we got back to the house.

CHAPTER 20

JEFFREY

The urge to flirt with Mindy was getting harder to resist. A few lines had slipped out despite my efforts. And when she'd looked up at me, so close that she was under the brim of my hat, I'd come close to asking her if she needed to be carried. Shoot, I'd just about kissed her. That was the opposite of not acting on my attraction.

A flash of clear thinking had kept me from tilting my head so that our lips met.

But I had to figure out what to say to her because I felt a we-need-to-talk conversation coming on. If I had to wager a guess, we wouldn't make it longer than a day before it came up.

"I should've stayed home like you asked, but I promise to stay in the truck and not cause trouble." She stared out the window, her hands tucked around herself.

"I'm not used to . . ." I inched along the dirt path, trying to figure out a different wording. "Here on the ranch, with the exception of Mad Dog, people do what I say. At the restaurant, I'm the boss."

"But I don't follow your orders."

"You have a mind of your own, and . . ." And I found it maddeningly attractive. I'd spent so much time with women who didn't seem to have opinions, or at least they didn't share them with me. My sister not included, but she didn't count. "I'm having to adjust." I pulled my gaze away from the path to see her expression. "It's not a bad thing."

She grabbed my arm. "Stop the truck!"

Thankfully, I wasn't going fast, and the truck stopped quickly with minimal skidding. But I should've been watching the road, not looking at Mindy. A tree, weighted down with ice and snow had fallen, blocking the path. To the left and right were trees, so if I was going to check on the cattle, the tree needed to be moved.

"Here. You'll need these." She pulled her hands out of my gloves.

Slipping them on, I slid out of the truck. The tree wasn't huge, but it wasn't exactly small. I grabbed a large branch on the heavier end and lifted. Getting it off the ground was one thing. Moving it was a different matter entirely.

The truck door opened. "I'm stronger than I look. Let me help."

"See if you can lift that end." I wasn't going to turn down an offer to help.

She used her legs to lift, and the trunk inched up off the ground. We managed to move it a short distance before I lost my grip.

"Sorry. Between the weight and the ice, I'm having trouble lifting it."

Standing with her hands on her hips, she pursed her lips. "What if . . ." Her gaze moved to the truck. "Do you have any rope or chain?"

"Of course."

"You could tether the tree to the truck and move it that way. If you tied one end to the bumper or grill or wherever, then backed up, there might be enough room to go around it."

"Yeah." I dug through the toolbox mounted in the bed of the truck. "Great idea. It's a good thing I brought you along."

Laughter rang out. Maybe if I spent all my time trying to make her laugh, I'd avoid saying something that would make both our lives awkward.

Once we'd securely attached the tree to the truck, I pointed at her. "Hop in. You back it up. Slowly. And I'll guide it in the right direction and signal you."

She blinked. "You want me to drive your truck?"

"Yes, because I want this big hunk of wood out of my way."

Before climbing in, she walked up to me. "What signals?"

I ran through the basic hand motions—back, left, right, and most importantly, stop.

"Okay. Got it." She pursed her lips as she climbed behind the wheel, then put the truck in reverse and inched it backward.

In no time at all, the tree was on the side of the dirt road, leaving us plenty of room to go around it.

The moonlight highlighted her grin. "We did it."

"Yep. Now let's get the cattle fed so we can warm ourselves in front of the fire."

I stepped toward her side of the truck, and she shook her head.

"Don't take the time to open my door. Just get in."

We bumped along the road toward the pasture, and when cows came into view, she leaned forward.

"Do you need my help feeding them?"

"Actually, yeah. Once we're in the gate, I'll climb into the back. We'll open this little window so you can hear me, and you can drive while I throw out hay and feed cubes."

"Sure."

I'd done this alone many times, but her coming along had saved so much time. The company was nice too.

～

SIR LANCELOT LAY SPRAWLED on the rug in a spot that was most decidedly warm. He looked content, which made Mindy happy. And in turn, that had me pleased as pie.

Mindy held out her hands near the fire. "Thank you for inviting me over. This is so much better than a pile of blankets."

"I wasn't going to let you freeze. I'm going to make myself some hot chocolate. You don't drink milk, I'm guessing. I have tea if you'd like a cup."

"Hot chocolate would be wonderful. Mind if I look at the box?"

"You can, but I made sure it was okay." When I'd shopped in preparation for the storm, I'd picked up a brand labeled gluten-free. Just in case. I hadn't planned for us to be stranded together, but maybe deep inside, I'd hoped something like this would happen.

I turned on the flame for one burner and set the teapot on to heat. While that came up to temp, I poured cocoa packets into two mugs, then poked my head into the den. "Want marshmallows?"

"Please." She crossed the room and followed me to the kitchen. "Some marshmallows aren't gluten-free, but the most common brands in the grocery stores are now."

"It's shocking all the places gluten is hiding."

She rested her hip against the counter. "I was in my twenties when I was diagnosed with celiac. It was a hard transition. And alienating. Back then, it wasn't popular to eat gluten-free, so nothing was labeled that way in restaurants. That made it very hard to eat out with friends.

Asking to read the chip bags at parties earned me strange looks."

"I'm sorry."

She rubbed at a spot on the counter. "I learned to deal."

Hearing her talk about the struggles was tugging at my heartstrings, and it had been a while since those strings had even been plucked. "I'm guessing it's easier now since more places label their meals."

"It is, but I still eat at home most of the time. It's less trouble, but it is nice when places indicate on the menu what's safe."

"Since hearing you were celiac, I've been having the menu redone to make sure all the dishes are labeled. And I've been reading about what needs to be done to have a dedicated area in the kitchen." I filled the mugs with water and passed hers over. "I don't want anyone to feel like they can't eat at my restaurant."

She blinked, and I hoped she wasn't about to cry. "That's sweet."

This was a first. No one had ever called me sweet. "Let's go back where it's warm. I'll let you choose which couch you want." I pushed open the door to the den, appreciating that the room was cozy.

"It's convenient that you have two couches."

"That one is usually in my office." I skipped telling her I'd moved it hours before the power was out.

She dropped onto the sofa farthest from the fire. "Thanks for going to all the trouble."

"No trouble." I sipped my cocoa.

"When Lilith hired me, I went home and looked up all the names she'd mentioned. I wanted to know the people I'd be working with." Mindy pulled a blanket over her legs.

"If you're cold, you can have this couch. It's warmer here."

"Okay." She walked over and sat on the far end closest to

the fire. When I started to push off the sofa, she shook her head. "You don't have to get up right now. Finish your chocolate."

"You were saying." I had a good idea about where this line of conversation was headed.

"The things I read about you. The opinion I formed before meeting you. That doesn't match who you seem to be. I'm sorry I was rude when we met." She eyed me over the rim of her mug. "And I'm not saying that so you'll . . ."

"So I'll what?"

"React a certain way. Those posts are wrong, but I believed them."

"What you read *was* true, but I've made different choices lately." That was the first step in explaining why I wouldn't pursue her, but I'd get to that eventually. The unexpectedly open and honest conversation was pleasant, but it was also ramping up all my feelings.

"Another thing I need to say."

"Uh-oh." I feigned horror, which drew a laugh.

"It's not bad. Well, it kind of is, but as long as I'm being chatty, I might as well tell you everything." Her voice cracked.

I scooted closer. "Hey. You okay?"

Nodding, she swallowed. "When I walked into your restaurant, my mouth started watering. The aromas wafting from the kitchen made me miss . . ." She sucked in a breath, tears glistening in the lamplight.

Keeping my distance wasn't happening right now. I lifted the mug out of her hands and pulled her close. "What did it make you miss?"

"Eating meat."

"Mindy, if you want a steak, I'll make you one." I brushed at a tear on her cheek. "If you want meat, why don't you eat it?"

"There's another reason I don't eat at restaurants often." She leaned her head on my shoulder. "About five years ago, I started getting really sick, and I'd break out in hives. My face would swell, and I had a headache most of the time. It was worse than when I'd been diagnosed with celiac. After several doctor visits, I was eventually diagnosed with Alpha-gal syndrome. At some point, I was bitten by a tick and developed an allergy to all mammal meats. Thankfully, I tolerate dairy and eggs."

Even the thought of a doctor giving me that diagnosis made me ill. "And I was not kind with my response when you told me you were a pescatarian."

"You didn't know." She wiped her face and pulled away from me.

"If someone dangled a steak in front of me but I couldn't eat it, I'd be perpetually grumpy."

Finally, she awarded me a smile. "I believe that."

"You said you were a pescatarian, but what about chicken and turkey and other fowl? Do you eat that?"

"I'm not allergic to it, but growing up, I loved everything about Thanksgiving except the turkey. I imagine my shoes might've tasted better. And whenever I've had chicken, it doesn't taste good. Even when I cooked it on my own. So I don't eat it."

I ran through recipes in my head. I could make chicken taste good, but I wanted to make her something amazing.

She poked my side. "I see your wheels turning. I didn't tell you any of that expecting you to fix the problem. You can't."

"What if I make you a chicken dish that isn't dry and will make your mouth water whenever you think about it?"

"What if I don't like it? I feel like that would be a horrible insult." She picked up the cup and held it in front of her as if it were a tiny shield.

"I won't be insulted. I'd just try making you something else. Please."

"Okay, but not tonight. I ate earlier, and I'm tired."

"Deal." I stood and stretched. "If you want to change in here, go ahead. I'll change in the other room and knock before I come back in."

"Thanks." She tracked my movement through the room and stood as I reached the door.

I'd just offered to cook for her. Now I had to justify why that wasn't an issue. I cooked for my sister all the time. But my feelings about Mindy were nothing like how I felt about Stephanie. Friends. Mindy and I were neighbors and friends.

How could I shake the desire to be more?

I'd have to think about that while I hauled her groceries over to my place.

CHAPTER 21

MINDY

I opted not to layer leggings and a long-sleeved shirt under my fleece jammies. The fire was warm, and I could add layers without embarrassment. Shedding layers was a different story.

The glow of firelight danced on the walls as Jeffrey shifted on his couch.

"Thank you for handling the groceries. I would've helped."

"It wasn't any trouble."

I dangled my hand near the floor. "Sir, come here, baby. Want to cuddle up?"

The cat usually slept with me, at least until he jumped out of bed in the middle of the night to chase phantoms. Hopefully he wouldn't do that tonight.

Sir yawned and stretched, then plodded toward the couches. Instead of jumping on top of me, that cat hopped up next to Jeffrey.

It was bad enough that I was basically throwing myself at the man, but now my cat was invading his space.

"Sir, leave the poor man alone. He doesn't want you crawling all over him."

"He's fine. I don't mind." Jeffrey settled on his side, and Sir nestled in beside him.

Wasn't this just the perfect picture? My cat curled up next to a cowboy. They made calendars with these kinds of pictures. Except Jeffrey had a shirt on. Thankfully.

My honest confessions hadn't been intended to spark romance between us, but I had thought it might move us past the being-friends-and-then-avoiding-each-other cycle we'd been in. It wasn't like we could avoid each other right now, but after Jeffrey made the offer to make me food, he might as well have been on Mars.

The most he'd said after changing clothes were the five words about the cat.

How was I going to sleep? It had taken me days after moving to achieve a solid night's rest because I wasn't good at falling asleep in unfamiliar places. Hotel stays were the worst. Every noise sparked a new train of thought.

This was no different. Besides the unfamiliar place, there was a man a few feet away. Based on the rhythm of his breathing, he wasn't sleeping either.

My phone buzzed, and I lunged for it, happy for something to do other than staring at the shadows.

Stephanie: Just checking on you. Do you still have power?

If she was asking if I had power, then she hadn't talked to Jeffrey since it went out. Either that or he'd failed to mention it.

Me: No power. You?

Stephanie: We still have it, but I've heard of several people who are without. Warm enough?

I was plenty warm thanks to the fireplace, but I wasn't sure telling Stephanie that I was staying with her brother was a great idea. But if I didn't tell her, she might worry.

Me: Jeffrey invited me to stay in his den. I've never been so happy to see a fireplace.

Stephanie: Oh, good. He's a great guy, Mindy.

I didn't disagree, so I sent a thumbs-up. Then I scrolled through my other messages. How had I missed so many?

Lilith: How are you doing? This weather is wild.

Joji: We still have power. If yours goes out, you can come here.

Joji: But I'm not sure how bad the roads are.

Ava: Do you have enough food? I can have Mad Dog take stuff over to you in the morning.

Tandy: I'm worried about you all alone in that cold house. Let me know you're okay. I'm not okay because I'm all alone too. LOL

There were several other messages from each of the ladies, and I tapped out replies to each of them, letting them know I was safe and warm at Jeffrey's.

Telling Tandy about my overnight stay invited comments and questions I didn't want, but I also didn't want her to be concerned. People didn't need to worry themselves about me.

Jeffrey dragged his large hand down the length of Sir's back. "That's a lot of typing over there."

"I'm answering texts. Your sister messaged, and then I noticed I'd missed a lot of texts." I set the phone on the table. "Sorry I bothered you."

"Why do you say things like that?"

"Like what?"

"You aren't a bother. *Ever.*"

His eyes were closed, but he could probably feel me staring at him. I'd been made to feel like a bother in the past, and it had shaped my thinking of myself. I wasn't even sure how to respond.

"Before you go to sleep, you should probably plug in your phone so it's fully charged in the morning. We don't know what tomorrow will bring." He motioned toward the outlet. "The generator provides power to these outlets."

I winced as my bare feet touched the ice-cold tile. After plugging in the charger, I hurried back to my couch, and Jeffrey's eyes snapped closed as soon as I looked his way. Sharing the den wouldn't be awkward at all.

The buzzing started again, and I slid out from under my blanket to check my phone. It wasn't my phone being pummeled with messages.

"Someone really wants to talk to you, it seems." Jeffrey rolled to his back and draped an arm over his face.

"I think it's you." Snuggling under the covers, I realized how that sounded. "I mean I think it's your phone that's buzzing. I didn't have any messages. And they might be messaging because they know we're without power and sleeping in the den."

He groaned as he stood. "Could be." He scrolled through his phone, but he didn't respond to the texts.

When he lay down again, keeping my mouth shut was impossible. "You aren't answering them?"

"Nope."

"Who messaged you?"

"Half the county, including my sister, Mad Dog, Beau, Clint, and Tandy. But she only asked if I'd do a snow angel shirtless for her."

I slapped a hand over my mouth, trying to stifle my laugh. Even with all her inappropriate remarks and questions, I loved that lady.

"You think that's funny?" He stretched out again, and Sir reclaimed his spot.

"Very. Are you going to do it?"

"Only if you're the one taking pictures."

My gasp was involuntary.

"Crap, Mindy. I'm sorry. I shouldn't have said that. I

just . . ." He flopped that arm over his face again. "We should sleep."

As if there was any chance I'd be getting any sleep after that comment.

I wasn't flirted with often. I'd been told I gave off an icy vibe, and apparently that deterred men. But Jeffrey's comment was unmistakably flirting.

Why had he been so quick to retract it?

Sir's purring and the crackle of the fire kept away the silence. I tried to figure out why Jeffrey would say that and immediately apologize until my brain hurt. Then I faced the back of the sofa, pulled the blankets over my shoulder, and closed my eyes. I needed to sleep.

What I wanted was something else entirely.

I OPENED my eyes and tried to be silent as I shifted to see if Jeffrey was awake. His couch was empty. After pulling on my fuzzy socks—because I had no desire to have my bare feet on that tile again—I picked up my phone to check the time. I couldn't remember the last time I'd slept past eight.

After wiping sleep out of my eyes, I noticed the text from Jeffrey.

Jeffrey: I'm headed out to do morning chores. Breakfast is in the oven. If the timer goes off before I return, get it out and help yourself.

The friendly message was a pleasant surprise after last night. I wasn't sure what I'd wake up to. And he hadn't even bothered telling me to stay in the house.

He'd messaged nearly an hour ago, but I wasn't going to start worrying yet.

Me: Text me if you need me to come rescue you.

Jeffrey: I'm in the kitchen.

Me: Those can be dangerous places.

Jeffrey: You have no idea. I'll be in with breakfast in a sec.

I ran my fingers through my hair. This is when I missed having it long. I would've had it knotted on top of my head. And of all the things I thought to throw in my bag, a brush wasn't one of them. I didn't feel like bundling up to walk to the house just to grab a brush. Instead, I'd pretend I didn't look horrible.

The door swung open, and Jeffrey carried a tray to the table. "Coffee and baked omelets with a side of fruit."

"Wow. I didn't realize the stay included free breakfast. I might have to sleep here more often."

When Jeffrey dropped his fork, it dawned on me how it must've sounded, and I slapped a hand over my mouth. "I didn't mean it like . . . you know, *that.*"

He nodded and sat as far away from me as possible. "Eggs, cheese, and veggies. I thought you were okay with all those."

"Yep." I sipped my coffee, then bit into the muffin-shaped breakfast. "This is so good. I love omelets, but I rarely take the time to make them. Do these freeze well?"

"They do. I usually keep a half dozen or so in the freezer. They are fast and easy to heat in the morning."

"Will you show me how you made them?" I loved learning new recipes, and so far, everything he'd made me tasted amazing. Granted, everything included a sandwich, hot cocoa, and breakfast, but I was impressed.

"Sure." He stood and carried his empty plate and mug toward the door. "I'll be outside checking on a few things."

"Do you need my help?"

"Nope." The door closed behind him, and I didn't see the man for hours.

CHAPTER 22

JEFFREY

*E*very part of me was cold, but staying busy outside was safer than being inside with Mindy. I tucked the broom away after sweeping the barn. Until today, I'd forgotten we kept a broom in here.

Beauty and Beast had both been fed, and I'd checked on the cows three times today. I think they'd rolled their eyes the last time I'd driven into the pasture.

I needed something else to do or else I might sweep Mindy into my arms. I wanted to kiss her and hug her and snuggle with her by the fire.

Fire required wood.

There was still a large pile, but it had shrunk. I could replenish what we'd used. I grabbed the axe. One by one, I split logs. Swinging the axe warmed me, and I shed my coat.

The sun sank toward the horizon, and after chopping a few more, I needed to carry this all inside and make us dinner.

I stood a log on end and lifted the axe.

"We need to talk." Mindy stood with her arms crossed. "But go ahead and finish your manly avoidance."

"We need wood for the fire."

She pointed to a stack nearly as tall as she was. "I'm pretty sure they don't expect the freeze to last until July."

"Look, Mindy, I've been out here because—"

"It's not your turn to talk." With her jaw set, she stared at the ground for several heartbeats before looking at me. "I'm not going to throw myself at you if you go into the house. I told you that my comment about sleeping here came out wrong. Do I find you attractive? Yes. There may not be a woman in Texas who wouldn't agree with me, but I get that you aren't interested. That's fine. We're adults, and I *thought* we were friends. So please explain to me why you prefer being out in eight-degree weather than inside with me." Her chest heaved, and she blinked, tears freezing to her lashes. "Despising you made it easier to keep my attraction in check, but then you had to go and call a truce. Besides, disliking you is difficult. But whatever this is, I can't do it. Maybe your reputation as a heartbreaker still applies."

I was caught between the horror of seeing her cry and the thrill of knowing she found me attractive. But both of those things only made the situation worse. After dropping the axe, I rubbed my face. "Hearing you talk about attraction only makes this harder. And, no, you aren't the type of woman I used to date. Young, short, and curvy describes most of those ladies. And giggly. The only thing you have in common with them is being young." The chill permeated my layers, and I put my coat back on. "I'm not that guy anymore. I don't date women twenty years younger. I can't. Arbitrary as it may be, I decided that fifteen years was the biggest gap acceptable. If I give on one thing, all my changes are in danger of eroding. And I won't let that happen. I'm very attracted to you, but I've been trying to squelch it and just be friends. And I've been doing a crap job. I'm sorry."

With her mouth open, she stared at me.

"I'm sorry I've made it awkward. I enjoy being around you, and I never meant for you to be hurt. Breaking your heart was never my intention. *Never.*" I hated the heart-breaker label, but even more, I hated that I'd made it true again.

Her head wagged back and forth; then she turned and walked away.

I'd blown it. Big-time. Detonating a friendship while trapped together wasn't the smartest thing I'd ever done. If I pulled in a space heater, I could survive a night in the barn.

I closed my eyes and rubbed my forehead. I felt like I'd been run through a shredder. Her hurt was likely worse.

My eyes popped open when she stepped right in front of me.

Her crossed arms were like a wall between us. "There are so many things wrong with what you said. First of all"—she held up one finger—"you aren't in your sixties. I looked you up, remember? So find a better excuse. And second, age shouldn't matter."

I inched closer. "Doesn't matter, huh? If I'd been dating a twenty-one-year-old when we met, what would you have thought of me?"

She moved back. "Maybe it matters a little."

"How old are you?" I'd completely lost my mind and was asking a woman about her age.

"Forty-two." She cocked her head and lifted her eyebrows as if she were daring me to argue with her.

"You're sure?" The question sounded stupid when I heard it out loud. But I used the time it took her to answer to confirm the math. Fourteen years.

She scrunched up her nose, and it was adorable. "The temps have frozen your brain. Yes, I'm sure of how old I am."

"You look younger." One of my reasons for holding back had been blown away by the truth. "I thought you were thirty-five." I'd also thought Mindy's friendship with Stephanie was a reason to avoid anything, but if I didn't act on my attraction because of my sister, she'd be more than a little upset.

"I'm not, but it's nice of you to say that." Mindy stuffed her hands in her pockets.

When I stepped toward her, she didn't move, and soon, we were as close as we'd been last night when I'd stopped her fall.

"Mindy."

"Yes." Her voice sounded breathy and full of expectation. She wasn't asking a question; she was giving me permission.

Pulling her close, I pressed my lips to hers. She gripped my coat and tugged me closer.

Standing outside in the cold, we made up for the month of repressed desire.

After a couple of minutes, she broke the kiss and touched a hand to my cheek. "So you were flirting last night."

"I slipped. You have no idea how many things I didn't say this past month, how many flirtatious comments I bit back."

"I believed those posts were true, but then at some point, I started hoping they weren't." She dropped her forehead to my shoulder. "I can't believe this."

I skimmed my lips on her ear. "You mean that it's snowing again?"

"Yes. That's exactly what I mean. If this keeps up, we're going to be stuck here for a week."

I swept her up into my arms and laughed when she squealed. "I don't see a problem with that."

She snuggled closer. "But eventually we'd run out of propane."

"I'm quite sure we could figure out other ways to stay warm." I carried her inside, all the way to the den. "I want to sit here and kiss you, but after skipping lunch, I'm starved.

Can we break for dinner, then resume snuggling and kissing?"

"I never imagined the Cowboy Chef as a snuggler." She lifted my cowboy hat off my head. "And my cooking isn't near as good as yours, but I made dinner. It should be ready—"

The oven timer sounded on cue.

"Now." Delight and desire twinkled in her blue eyes.

"I look forward to tasting whatever you've cooked up."

Her lips brushed against mine. "You can make almost anything sound like flirting."

"I have other talents too."

"In the kitchen. I remember." She traced a finger along my bottom lip.

If it weren't for the stupid oven timer's repeated beeping, I'd have stayed hungry a bit longer.

Being stranded because of snow and dealing with a power outage wasn't so horrible. It had forced the honest conversation—no thanks to me—and it was clear Mindy was everything I never knew I wanted.

I PULLED ON MY COAT. "I need to go make sure the troughs don't have ice on top." After leaning in to kiss her, I zipped my coat. "Want to come with me?"

"I thought you were going to tell me to stay put."

With an arm around her waist, I tugged her close. "We both know how well that works."

"Let me throw on an extra layer and get my boots on." After a few steps, she turned around. "I haven't dated anyone in a very long time. And I thought—I don't know exactly— but that it would be more awkward, that I'd be unsure about what to say."

"But this feels natural, and you don't have to filter yourself with me. Part of your charm is you tell it like it is." I loved that about her. Women with opinions were much more entertaining than I'd ever imagined.

With her arms folded, she stared at the floor. "Have you told anyone?"

"Didn't think it was anyone else's business."

She smiled. "Give me two minutes."

No one had to lecture me about what a treasure I'd found in Mindy, and I had no plans to take advantage of that. What did surprise me was how vulnerable she'd been.

Protecting that tender part of her was imperative. I couldn't mess this up.

CHAPTER 23

MINDY

Stretched out on the sofa, Jeffrey opened his arms, and I snuggled against him and rested my head on his chest. The fire crackled, and Sir jumped up to join us. "I know you were a bad boy who's been trying to be good, but tell me something else about you."

"Bad might be an exaggeration."

I lifted my head to meet his gaze. "I'm not sure about that, but it doesn't matter now."

"I wish more people agreed with you." He ran his fingers through my hair. "That's the thing about reputations. You can set it aside and try to walk away, but someone always, always chases you down to hand it back. It's like when you get a truly awful gift at the office party, and no matter how hard you try, you can't get out the door without someone reminding you not to forget it."

"I'm sorry I handed it back."

Warm fingers grazed my cheek. "The way you reacted to me when we met is not all that uncommon. But then there are other women who assume I'm still that person, and they blatantly flirt, thinking I want the attention."

"I saw some of that at the New Year's Eve party."

"You don't know how close I came to kissing you that night. When you walked in there to distract the agitated Chuck, I was furious. Then you told me why, and I melted."

After pressing a quick kiss to his cheek, I put my head down again. "And then you avoided me."

"Yep, but we don't need to rehash that."

"I understand about having boundaries, Jeffrey. But did you ever think maybe the reasons for wanting to date someone were just as important?"

He kissed the top of my head. "I didn't trust myself not to rationalize."

"Then it's a good thing I'm as old as I am. Now tell me something else about you."

Laughter rumbled in his chest as he turned his head and stared at the fire. "Owning a restaurant has been my dream for a long time. I worked at a few other places. Then I had a food truck for a while, but the stuff I make isn't well suited to that format."

Drawing circles on his shirt, I listened as he told me more about who he was, what he wanted.

"The winery grew in popularity, and Stephanie suggested I open a restaurant there. It was the best decision I've ever made." He leaned down and kissed my head again. "Maybe not *the best* one."

"You're flirting again."

He could probably read a menu aloud and make it sound seductive and alluring.

He chuckled, and I loved the way the sound echoed in his chest.

"I have plans to expand the restaurant, but I'm waiting until I can justify the cost. We're getting there."

It took all my willpower not to mention Donna's planned

visit. If it fell through, I didn't want Jeffrey to be disappointed. "I'd like to eat there one night."

"Just say when. I'll make you the best seafood you've ever tasted. I've been adding more seafood options to the menu." His hand moved out of my hair and down my back. "What do you do when you aren't planning parties and events?"

"I read and cook. Pretty boring stuff."

"Hey now. You just described my life, so be nice." The firelight reflected in his green eyes, making him even more striking.

"But you also garden."

"And that makes me sound like a regular party animal." He poked my side. "But soon we'll go out one night. I'll take you dancing."

"I haven't been dancing in a long time, but that sounds wonderful."

Our lips spent a few minutes celebrating the idea of a night out, and when he broke away, Jeffrey grew serious. "I've been curious about something."

"What?" It still shocked me that Jeffrey had been attracted to me this whole time.

"If it's something you'd rather not talk about it, just say so."

"Ask me."

"Where did you go for Christmas? You haven't mentioned any family, and . . ." He stayed quiet for a full second. "I thought maybe you had someone serious in your life."

"That's nothing to worry about. There is a prince of this tiny land-locked country who comes to the States every year or so, and we spend a few days together. It's not serious or anything." I struggled not to laugh.

He poked me again. Then his fingers wiggled against my side.

I wriggled. "Okay. I'll tell you."

His arms tightened around me. "No. Keep your secrets, darling. And I'll keep mine."

"Very funny. No thank you. I was with some friends. We all went to college together and have stayed in touch since. They're all married now, and we don't get together as often." I patted his chest. "Happy?"

"When do I get to meet them?"

Instead of answering him, I stretched up and kissed him. His question made it clear that for him this wasn't a few stolen moments because we were stranded. And as much as I wanted this to be real, the thought that he was taking advantage of the situation had been worming its way through my brain all evening.

"I liked that answer." His hand trailed up and down on the back of my sweatshirt.

"I'll see when they're free. Showing them an actual ranch would be fun. And I haven't mentioned family because it's just me. I was an only child, and my parents both died pretty young." My friends were the closest thing I had to family now, and they'd be so excited I'd found him. Although my family was expanding now that I worked at the venue.

"I'm sorry about your parents. That must've been hard." His condolence was soft and simple, but he knew how it felt to lose parents. He knew there wasn't anything to say that could make it better. Simple acknowledgement meant more than lots of flowery words.

"I liked seeing you with your sister. Y'all are lucky to have each other."

"As far as sisters go, she's a good one. And I'm glad y'all met. It seems like you hit it off."

"I like her. We got together a couple of times during the weeks you were avoiding me. Also, she's a big fan of yours. Not sure if she's told you that, but she's mentioned what a gem you are a few times and also told me to be patient with you." And when she'd said that, I'd smiled rather than rolling my eyes because it hadn't occurred to me she'd picked up on Jeffrey's interest. I'd been oblivious.

"This is the way it's going to be, isn't it? We'll be having heartfelt conversations, and you'll slide in a reminder of how wrong I was."

"I'll be good." I flashed my sweetest smile.

The lights flickered, then stayed on. Just when I wanted it to stay out, the power came back on.

I pushed up. "And we have lights again."

He kept his arms around me. "Stay."

It had been below freezing longer than we'd been an item. For me, it was too soon for more than kissing. "But we've barely . . ." I swallowed the lump in my throat. "I'm not ready to—"

"I'm not asking for more than this because you're right. It's too soon." He brushed a thumb on my cheek. "But there are still two couches in here."

"When you put it that way. And I'm not sure Sir will be happy about leaving. He likes you better."

"I think he sleeps on me for the warmth."

"Smart cat. You are warm. That's one more thing I like about you."

He kissed me again.

I'd probably be up late, and I didn't mind at all.

CHAPTER 24

JEFFREY

The power was still on when I woke up, which was good. It had also started snowing again, which was also good. Neither of us were leaving the ranch until the weather changed.

It was early, and chores needed to be done, but right now, I was happily admiring Mindy. Things had moved at warp speed yesterday. At least it had for me. Nothing happened that would make anyone blush, but emotionally—which was not something I often talked about—it felt fast. I needed to steady the pace. I was embarking on new territory, and I wanted to do it right.

Her eyes fluttered open. She could probably sense me staring at her, which admittedly was a tad creepy. So, I looked away.

Then she shifted, and my gaze jumped back to her.

"Morning." With a sleepy smile spread across her face, she stretched her arms above her head and yawned. "Sleep well?"

"I did. You?"

Nodding, she stood and folded her blanket. "Your couch is comfortable."

"Good. You're welcome anytime. I'll even throw in breakfast." I walked up to her and pulled her close. "I like you, Mindy. I admire your spunk, your honesty—though it's sometimes brutal—and your figure. I probably shouldn't have mentioned that last one. You'll think I've reverted to my old ways."

A blush crept up her cheeks. "I dreamt last night that this"—she moved her hand back and forth between us—"was all a dream, so when I got up, I kept the conversation neutral until I was sure."

To confirm this bliss wasn't a dream, I pressed my lips to hers, and she melted against me. I'd never tire of that. "I guess I'll have to show up at your door every morning and kiss you so you know I'm real." I clasped her hand and led her into the kitchen.

She leaned on the counter. "Sounds like a perfect plan. I should call Lilith. I doubt there is anything happening today, but just in case."

I pulled back the curtain. "I doubt anyone is on the roads."

"Snowing again? Maybe you should do that snow angel." She pulled mugs out of the cabinet.

"For you, sweetheart, I'd do it. Just to hear that musical laugh."

She slapped a hand over her mouth, trying to stifle a laugh. "You flirt and tease so much, I don't always know when you're serious."

I started the coffee brewing. "I think the real problem is, you aren't used to someone flirting with you. I plan to change that."

A pink tint colored the apples of her cheeks as she smiled.

"What if I warm some of the baked omelets for breakfast? Then we'll get chores done."

"Sure. And after that will you teach me some of your cooking magic?"

I'd never had a woman show genuine interest in my cooking. Some raved about the end product. Some picked at it and pretended they were eating because what I'd made didn't fit with their current fad diet.

"I'd like that."

She ran a finger around the rim of her mug. "I know it's a bit difficult to cook for me because of all the things I can't have, so if you'd rather not, I understand."

Leaving the food on the counter, I squatted in front of her. "Mindy, look at me."

Her gaze lifted, but her head stay tilted down. "You don't have to go to a lot of trouble for me. You can even just tell me how you do things, and I'll take notes."

This conversation was going to take longer than my knees were prepared to be in this position. "Hold that thought."

Her brow furrowed a little, but she sipped her coffee, watching as I warmed our breakfast.

I set our food on the table, dragged a chair next to her, and sat down. "I'm not going to pretend to understand what you've been through with trying to avoid all those foods. And I wasn't nice when you mentioned being a pescatarian."

"I think maybe you were reacting more to my insult."

"You think? But it's not a good excuse. For all the times you've felt ostracized or alienated because of your allergies, I'm sorry. As much as I'd like to snap my fingers and make everything better, I can't fix that."

"I'm not asking you to fix it, Jeffrey." She rested her hand on mine. "But after I suggested cooking today, I worried I'd asked for too much."

"That group of friends, do they find restaurants where you can eat? Or make sure what they're serving is something you can have?"

A smile accompanied her nod. "Yes. It's part of the reason

we've been friends so long, I think. With them, I never felt like a burden. Well, until recently. I feel like a burden being the only single woman in the group."

"I want to be that kind of friend. The kind of friend who makes sure you aren't left hungry while others eat."

Her gaze flitted from me to her plate. "Okay."

There was that word again.

Trailing a finger down her arm, I leaned in close. "I want to be more than a friend. Obviously. I *hope* I've made that obvious."

"You have. I just . . ." She picked up her fork, then set it down. "It's new."

There was more she wasn't saying, but I wasn't going to push her. She didn't like standing out. That had been my role most of my life.

"I'm proud of the fact that I can cook. I'm good at what I do. You can eliminate whatever ingredients you want, and I'll still make you something amazing. That's what I do."

"Like a cooking challenge." She started eating, and I relaxed a bit.

The snow had come at a good time because being together without others around was helpful, needed even. We had time for talking, cooking, and doing more of what we'd done last night.

The most surprising part of all this was that Mindy believed I'd changed. I had, but convincing people of that wasn't easy.

AFTER PUTTING stuff away in the barn, I walked outside and was hit square in the chest with a snowball.

"Hey!" I reached down and gathered snow into a clump.

This was a side of Mindy I hadn't anticipated. Since

breakfast, she'd been chatty, and this was downright playful. I was starting to love the contradiction that was Mindy.

Laughing, she braced for retaliation, the poof on the top of her winter hat wiggling back and forth. She raised her arm to throw another before I finished getting a snowball ready.

"Were you prepping ammo while I was inside working?" I tossed one, and she dodged, but not enough, so it skimmed her hip.

She threw two more, proving herself to be a better shot than I was. "Yep." Then she turned and wiggled her backside. "You aren't a good throw."

With a target like that, how could I miss? It wasn't big, but I'd have no trouble keeping my gaze fixed on it.

After tossing snow at each other for a half hour, I scooped her up. "I'm getting hungry. It's time for your first cooking lesson."

She rested her head on my shoulder. "What are we making?"

"Your choice—chicken or seafood."

Her brow pinched in the middle. "You won't be upset if I don't like it?"

"Not a bit. It'll only ramp up the challenge."

She swung the door closed after we'd cleared the doorway. "That's the way you operate, isn't it? There are no roadblocks, only detours." Leaning closer to my ear, she whispered, "Also, I really like that you can carry me."

"I may be old, but you're thin, so it works. And yes, life is full of detours. That's what makes it interesting. Detours have taken me places I'd never even thought of going. And I loved it."

Once she was on her feet, she shrugged out of her coat. "Teach me, O Great One."

"No kissing while we cook. I don't want the distraction."

Mindy had never been good at adhering to my orders, and I hoped this was time would be no different.

She shrugged. "Can't promise anything."

"The first thing I'm going to show you is a secret. Only one other person on this planet knows the recipe for my secret spice, and Stephanie might've forgotten it already."

Mindy violated my edict, and I relished the distraction.

I pulled out ingredients, showing her the proportions for the spice mix. Once it was ready, I set it aside and got out the rest of what we'd need, then explained how we'd use each one and why.

This was a dish I could make with my eyes closed, but today, cooking took extra focus because I noticed every touch from Mindy.

But the expression on her face when she took the first bite made me feel like I'd won a trophy. "You like?"

"A lot." Her head bobbed up and down as she popped another bite in her mouth. "It's not chicken leather."

"Think you could make it if I weren't around?"

"Maybe."

Conversation died as she focused on her food, and I couldn't have been happier.

CHAPTER 25

*B*y late afternoon, temperatures were above freezing, and there was a constant dripping as snow and ice melted all over the ranch. That was the only sound as Jeffrey and I walked across the driveway to my house.

We were leaving our little snow globe and venturing back into real life. That had me on edge. Overthinking—my superpower—was ramping up with force.

He reached around me and opened the door. "I want to walk through and make sure no pipes burst."

"Sure."

He set my bag in a chair and strode down the hall.

I put Sir Lancelot on the sofa. "We're home, buddy."

"It all looks fine, but if you notice anything weird, call me." He stopped in front of me. "Did you get everything?"

"I think so, but if I forgot something, I promise not to knock on your door at two asking about it."

He slipped an arm around me waist. "I've never been so happy about being snowed in."

When he leaned in to kiss me, I tried shutting out all the

thoughts stabbing at my brain so I could enjoy it. Today and the evening before had been the closest thing to perfect I'd ever experienced, and since I'd been engaged once, that said something. But my pessimism was tired of being shushed.

Head tilted, he studied my face. "Everything okay?"

"Mostly. I'm thinking about all that's waiting for me at work." And how Lilith and Tandy are going to laugh when they discover I'd fallen for Jeffrey's charms.

"Ouch. I'm kissing you, and that's what you're thinking about? You're hard on my ego, darling."

"Your ego is fine." I inched up and pressed a quick kiss to his lips. "I guess I'll see you tomorrow."

"I'd offer you breakfast, but I'm leaving really early to check on things. Stephanie made sure the pipes didn't freeze, but I have cleanup and prep to do." He played with my hair. "I'll leave my door unlocked. Help yourself to whatever you want. There are some baked omelets left."

"Thank you." I rested my head on his shoulder as his arms tightened around me.

For a full second, he held me. Maybe he was also nervous about how we'd fare once life was back to normal.

Then he kissed my forehead and stepped toward the door. "Call me if you need anything. You know where to find me."

Once he was back in his house, I stepped away from the window and changed into jammies. Then I pulled out a cookie mix that only required water and oil. All my perishables were still in Jeffrey's fridge, but I'd get them tomorrow.

Baking cookies would keep me busy because if I crawled in bed now, I wouldn't sleep.

Overthinking was inevitable. Getting cookies out of the deal was a bonus.

∼

I STUFFED a cookie in my mouth and started the engine. By the time I'd driven the mile to the venue, I'd finished two more cookies.

The first to arrive, I slipped into my office. Only one event had been canceled, but I needed to contact them about rescheduling. My email was probably full of new requests since people had been cooped up at home.

After making myself coffee, I settled in to tackle emails and messages.

An hour later, the front door opened. "Hello!" Lilith poked her head into my office. "Let me get coffee; then we'll chat."

Hopefully the chat would be about work.

Cradling a mug, she dropped into a chair. "How was your stay at Jeffrey's?"

I knew these questions were coming. Why did they bother me? "It was good. Much warmer than the old house. And I think my cat likes Jeffrey more than me."

She laughed. "Princess—that's my cat—loves Beau because he feeds her whatever she wants. He talks about how cats belong in the barn; then he snuggles with Princess on the couch. Most adorable thing ever."

"I can imagine." I could imagine because Sir and Jeffrey had snuggled a lot during our short stay.

She sipped her coffee. "I'm glad you had someplace warm to ride out the freak storm. And sorry y'all lost power. It stayed on over here the whole time."

Should I be suspicious that nearly everyone I'd talked to never lost power? Surely Jeffrey wouldn't have faked it. I was with him when the power had come back on. The whole idea of his staging the outing was ridiculous. It bothered me that I'd entertained the idea.

"There are worse things than being stranded with a chef."

"I bet." Pushing up out of her chair, she shook her head. "I can't delay any longer. Work is calling."

For the next few hours, classic country music wafted through the office building as I worked. Lilith stayed in her office; I was in mine.

Then the door opened. "I'm here! And I brought goodies." Tandy sounded more chipper than I'd ever heard her.

Lilith called from her office, "Be out in a minute."

I walked out to the sitting area. "Hi. Goodies, huh?"

"I baked the whole time I was snowed in, but a woman can only eat so many cakes and cookies. These don't have any flour in them. You can have as many as you want, but first . . ." She crossed her arms and dropped into the easy chair. "Tell me about the kissing."

News clearly spread fast, but I hadn't been the source. That left one person, and it hurt that he'd announced his conquest so quickly. I felt duped.

The nice and sweet Jeffrey was just a cover for the charming and manipulative Jeffrey. He'd won me over. Was he off somewhere laughing with the guys?

Maybe he'd bet someone money that the icy Mindy could be melted. He'd discover she could just as easily refreeze.

"I have work to do." I spun around, far too angry to say more for fear of uttering words I'd regret. Making sure it didn't slam, I closed my office door and got back to work.

Last night's overthinking was my brain's way of trying to warn me. Why hadn't I listened?

JEFFREY'S TRUCK wasn't there when I arrived home, which was just as well. I didn't want to see him. I'd avoid him as long as possible. Then, I'd finally unload. But I needed time for my ice walls to solidify.

After grabbing a quick dinner, I hunted for my book. I was only a few chapters from finishing, but where was it? I'd taken it to Jeffrey's, but I'd picked it up when I packed. With my eyes squeezed closed, I replayed my actions. Then he'd snuck up behind me, and we'd ended up snuggled on the sofa. I hadn't seen the book since.

But now I didn't want to finish because the book made me think of Jeffrey.

I crawled into bed and closed my eyes. Instead of counting sheep, I counted cattle. The cows were sauntering past Jeffrey's truck one at a time. That wasn't helping me go to sleep.

At two in the morning, the familiar sound of Jeffrey's truck let me know he was home. I yanked the pillow over my head.

I would not cry about this.

But I couldn't sleep either.

Dozing off and waking up thinking someone was knocking filled the rest of my night.

When someone did knock, sunlight was pouring in the windows.

It had to be Jeffrey, but I wasn't ready to face him. Hiding under my covers, I avoided the confrontation.

Then my phone buzzed.

Jeffrey: Good Morning. I made breakfast. Gluten-free pancakes.

I stared at the phone. Either he was a master at deception, or I was wrong about him. If the error was on my part, that alone should be a signal. I didn't trust him. Relationships didn't work without trust.

Ignoring him would only make him more determined to see me.

Me: I can't today.

What I didn't say was that I wasn't sure if I ever could.

CHAPTER 26

JEFFREY

I read Mindy's text, seeing it for what it was.

I'd dated a lot and had been screamed at and ghosted nearly as much. Mindy wasn't busy. She was avoiding me.

Problem was, I didn't know why.

It was time for a detour.

Using a squeeze bottle, I added more pancakes to the griddle, pouring them into heart shapes. While those cooked, I picked out the most heart-shaped strawberries and cut them in half. Her themed breakfast would be delivered to her doorstep.

If she didn't want to see me, fine. But I'd make sure she thought of me every time she was hungry.

After flipping the pancakes, I whisked heavy cream until it was perfectly whipped.

Then I placed all the food into disposable containers with as much care about the presentation as I took plating food at the restaurant. I loaded it all into a paper sack, added a mini bottle of maple syrup, and set it outside her door. Once I was back inside, I texted her.

Me: Food is waiting outside your door. I hope you have a great day.

I waited a few heartbeats and then sent an emoji I'd never sent before, that little kissy one.

Any of my friends who saw it would think I'd completely lost it. I had. And whatever I'd messed up, I intended to fix. Somehow.

Sipping coffee, I stood near the window. Her door opened, and she looked around before picking up the bag. Her hair poked out in multiple directions, and I gripped the counter to prevent me from running over.

What bothered her so much she wouldn't unleash that particular brand of Mindy honesty on me?

Had someone said something that made her doubt me? I thought we'd moved past that, but maybe we hadn't. But what I felt with Mindy was worth fighting for. And I'd fight with kindness. And food. Food had made her feel isolated, and I'd use it to make her feel cared for.

But I'd let her avoid me a few days. When she was ready, then we'd talk. Once I knew what was wrong, I'd work on fixing it, no matter how many detours it required.

An idea struck me, and I dialed, setting my plan into action.

"Hello, Jeffrey. What's up?" Lilith had a suspicious edge to her voice.

No part of me was surprised that people would assume I'd fouled up. "I need a favor."

"What kind of favor?"

"You may already know this, and I don't want to get into nitty-gritty details, but Mindy is upset with me."

"I figured you were why she wasn't herself yesterday afternoon. What did you do?"

"That's the clincher. I have no clue. Mind if I ask about what happened yesterday?"

"Nothing happened. Mindy was in her office working. Then Tandy showed up, and—"

"Tandy. You don't need to say anything else." That woman lived on innuendos and stirring things up, and I had no doubt she was the reason for Mindy's change of heart. "Anyway, the favor."

"I have to know what it is before I agree."

"Mindy doesn't want to talk to me, but if you could let me know when she heads home, I'd like to have dinner delivered to her. To show her I'm not horrible."

"Are you going to deliver it?"

"No. I'll send my assistant. Scout's honor."

Laughter rang out. "Don't even pretend you're a Boy Scout."

"Ouch."

"She usually leaves around five on non-event days, and there isn't anything scheduled for today. I'll text you."

"Let me know when you're leaving, and I can have dinner sent to you too." I appreciated that Lilith trusted me enough to send the info.

"Maybe another night, but thanks. And Jeffrey . . ."

"Yeah?" I braced for the expected lecture on being careful with Mindy's heart.

"I'm rooting for you."

"That's appreciated. I think I'm going to need it." After ending the call, I peeked out the window.

Mindy's car was gone. Had she eaten the pancakes or were they in her trash? I'd probably never know.

MAD DOG KNOCKED AS he stepped inside. "Did you manage to keep everything alive while I was gone?"

"Almost everything." I poured him a cup of coffee.

"Uh-oh. That sounds ominous."

I nodded toward the table, then took a seat. "I need some advice. Maybe just some reassurance."

"Did things not go well while Mindy was here?"

"That's the thing. They went really well. No offense to all my other friends, but I can't imagine a better person to be stranded with. Mindy is incredible. Pretty. Funny. Caring. She's the whole package."

"I think that's great. It's not much of a surprise though. The sparks were obvious."

"Yeah, well, what's obvious now is that she's avoiding me. Deep down, I know I don't deserve someone like her, but I can't just give up without trying. I'm not the person I was. I'm not. I need her to believe that, and I'm not sure she does. Or if she ever will." I washed down the sour taste of those words with a gulp of coffee.

"I slept in the guest room after Ava and I got married."

"I remember."

"It felt like an eternity until that changed. But it did change."

I refilled my coffee. "Now is not the time to tell me about your love life."

"Show Mindy you care, in authentic ways, but give her time. It's not all about you. You assume it's because of your reputation, but she might have other reasons."

The advice was solid, actionable. "I can do that. I think."

"Mindy's lucky."

"How so?"

Mad Dog stood and set his hat on his head. "I'm guessing you are going to cook for her a lot. That's how you show love. Oh, and let me know if you want to shoot hoops later. I think I have other shoes in my truck. I've eaten my weight in sweets since I was here last. Ava baked while it snowed because having the oven on warmed the house."

I wasn't the only one who conveyed care with my cooking. "I'll take a raincheck." I'd be in the restaurant's kitchen, making Mindy's dinner. "Thanks for the chat."

He chuckled. "It's so fun when we talk about our feelings."

CHAPTER 27

MINDY

I couldn't bring myself to throw the breakfast away. It had been ages since I'd had pancakes, and they smelled so good. I'd brought the bag to work with me, and now I had to decide whether to eat what he'd made and risk losing my resolve or miss out on what I knew would be delicious.

When I pulled the lid off the heart-themed breakfast, I bit back a sob. I was ignoring a man who had no idea I was mad. Or maybe he did know and was trying to win me over. Assuming the latter was true, I cut into the pancakes.

Getting over Jeffrey would take a while, But I'd manage. I sure would miss his cooking though. At least I'd gotten one lesson.

"Morning." Lilith lifted her coffee cup in greeting. "What you got there? Smells good."

"Pancakes."

"Hearts! How fun. I couldn't believe how many items crept onto my to-do list yesterday. It'll be a busy month."

"Busy is good." Having work as an excuse would make it easier to avoid Jeffrey.

She stayed seated and sipped her coffee. "Don't let me stop you from eating. I already had breakfast. Ava has been baking up a storm—no pun intended—and she made eggs and bacon this morning. I'm stuffed." She rubbed her stomach. "Having friends who can cook is a wonderful thing."

That was poorly veiled.

"Yep." I drizzled more syrup on the stack.

"And you should take whatever Tandy said with a grain of salt." She stood and walked out of the room without even a look back.

Clearly, my emotional turmoil hadn't gone unnoticed. Lilith probably thought I was the most unprofessional employee ever. I'd have to make sure my personal stuff didn't interfere with my work life.

Thankfully, for at least the next month, Jeffrey wasn't scheduled to cater any events, but that could change. I hoped it didn't. At least not until I was ready to talk to him, which was the adult thing to do.

The sting was still too fresh. It was hard enough living across the driveway from him.

THAT AFTERNOON, I stared at my ringing phone. It wouldn't be fair to Stephanie to ignore her just because I didn't want to talk about Jeffrey.

After a deep breath, I answered. "Hello."

"Can you believe how crazy the weather was?"

"I thought that never happened around here." I forced a casual laugh. "Were you able to save the grapevines?"

"We did. It took some work, but I have a few employees who live here on the property, and they were a huge help. I know you're probably busy after being stuck, but when you have time, we should get together."

I wasn't going to retreat from friendships because of Jeffrey. "Sounds great. I'm free tonight."

"Perfect. Your place okay? I'll text when I'm headed that way."

"Sounds good. I'm looking forward to it."

We'd had an entire conversation, and Jeffrey's name hadn't come up at all. I appreciated that.

As I hung up, Tandy dropped into a chair in front of my desk. "I'm sorry."

"For what?"

"Running my mouth. It was obvious what I said bothered you, but I meant it in fun. It's great y'all fanned those flames so to speak." She leaned back and grinned. "I have to live vicariously through others. My life is boring. It's worse when my characters are quiet. You'd think I'd have finished an entire book while I was home, but no. I baked. Silly me."

It was hard to be mad at Tandy. "Don't worry about it."

"Life is too short for worry. Instead, I do something about it." She stood, and with her hands on her hips tilted backward in a stretch. "Anyway, I should go. Stuff to do and all that."

"Please, Tandy, don't try to fix anything."

She waved as she walked out of the office, and my gut knotted. Whatever she was planning would only make it worse.

I packed up, ready to head home a little early. My brain was too fried to get more work done right now, but I could work from my couch later tonight.

"Lilith, I'm leaving. If you need anything, just call or text." It seemed courteous to let her know when I was leaving, and maybe she wouldn't think I was moping in my office.

"All right. Have a nice evening. Have big plans tonight?"

She didn't mention Jeffrey, but I thought of him all the same.

"Nothing huge. Stephanie's coming over."

"Have fun." She slipped her readers back on and turned back to her computer.

I had to stop thinking that everyone was asking about Jeffrey. They were friendly before I'd fallen into his arm and against his lips.

Living a mile from work had its perks, and I was opening my front door in a matter of minutes. Sir blew past me as soon as he sensed freedom.

What was with this cat?

I dropped my purse on the counter and chased after him. "Sir Lancelot, come here."

At least this time Jeffrey wasn't watching me from the window.

Sir Lancelot was where I hoped he wouldn't be. In Jeffrey's herb garden.

"Quit digging there! Are you trying to get me in trouble?" I scooped up my muddy cat and patted down the dirt, hoping Jeffrey wouldn't notice his beloved herb garden had been disturbed.

If Sir kept this up, he'd make avoiding Jeffrey impossible.

I turned on the bathroom faucet and washed Sir's paws, which he absolutely hated. That would teach him to go digging in Jeffrey's dirt.

As soon as I put him down, he took off. I wouldn't see him for a while.

I needed to figure out dinner, so I opened the refrigerator. There wasn't much in there. I hadn't gone to get my groceries before deciding I didn't want to see Jeffrey.

Maybe something at the local barbecue place was safe. Turkey was on the menu, and after tasting Jeffrey's chicken, I was willing to try something new. I'd know if it wasn't safe when I ended up doubled over with abdominal pain. I hated that eating had to be complicated.

My phone beeped, and I turned off the sound before checking the message.

Stephanie: Don't cook. Dinner is covered.

Now I liked her even more.

CHAPTER 28

*T*he kitchen was hopping when Lilith texted.

Lilith: Your friend just left, and she headed toward your place, not away.

Me: I owe you.

Lilith: Yes, you do.

Lilith: And she's having company tonight.

Me: I'm aware.

Stephanie hadn't asked anything about how things had gone with Mindy, which I appreciated. She'd simply let me know she had plans with my neighbor this evening. I had a pretty great sister.

I made Mindy's dinner, being careful with every detail, then boxed it up and handed it to my assistant along with Stephanie's meal. "The address is here on the note. Please deliver these."

She read the sticky note and squinted. "That's where you live."

"You are taking it to the old house. It's written at the bottom." I pointed to the note. "Make sure you go to the front door. Not the one closest to the driveway."

"I think I can manage it."

"This has to go perfectly."

Laurel rolled her eyes. "What do you think I'm going to do? Drop it several times, then throw it at her back door? I can deliver food. And see how nice I'm being by not even asking about why you are having food delivered to your houseguest?"

"Who's been talking about me and my houseguest?"

"Who isn't? Rumors are swirling that you've finally met your match."

The only people not talking about Mindy and me were my friends and sister. I knew them well enough to know that. Tandy, on the other hand, I wasn't so sure about.

"Please don't add to the rumor mill."

She shook her head. "No worries. Rumors don't matter. I knew she'd nabbed you the first time she walked into your office." Laurel lifted the bag. "I better run before it gets cold."

I checked my phone every few minutes the rest of the night, but Mindy never messaged. I did get a text from my sister.

Stephanie: She liked it. And I made sure she knew it was from you.

Me: Thanks

When I arrived home at an ungodly hour, there was a note stuck to my door.

Thank you.

That was Mindy's handwriting. I counted that as a success.

I'D THOUGHT time dragged when I was avoiding Mindy, but it was so much worse when she avoided me. Five days without any sign of her changing her mind had me wondering if she'd ever speak to me. I'd left breakfast on her doorstep every morning and had dinner delivered every night.

And I'd reminded myself that it wasn't about me. She was hurting. I didn't know why. Even though stewing was now part of my daily routine, I let her continue to avoid me. Taking her food hopefully sent the message I was here and interested. Soon, I'd go talk to her. That had worked before, but right now, I had the distinct impression the *Welcome* on her doormat didn't apply to me.

The sun was just starting to sink low when I pulled through the gate and parked on my side of the driveway. Mindy drove in behind me and parked on her side. Then she sat in her car. While I was tempted to tilt my seat back and wait to see what she'd do, I opted to be nice.

I climbed out, waved at her, then walked into the house.

After hanging my keys on the hook, I wandered into the kitchen and took my time rolling up my sleeves and pulling out what I needed to get part of dinner started. The rice cooker could do its magic while I relaxed a bit.

I had halibut in the fridge that I'd hoped to make as a dinner for two, but it looked like I'd be dropping hers off outside her door. Again.

The den beat the kitchen when it came to stewing in comfort, so I went in there. I hit the switch to turn on the lights and chuckled. Mindy's sleek gray cat lay curled up on my sofa. Sir lifted his head and meowed, and I wasn't sure if it was intended as a greeting or an order to turn the lights back off.

"What are you doing here? Did someone teach you how to open doors?" I picked him up and stroked his fur. "She'll be worried sick when she discovers you're gone."

Thanks to the cat, I wouldn't have to wait any longer before talking to Mindy.

Mad Dog strolled up as I walked outside. "I'm headed home."

"Have a good one. I'm taking this fella back to Mindy. I'm not sure how he even got into my house."

"I let him in. He got out while Tandy was here, but he seemed determined to get into your place, and I figured it couldn't hurt anything." He opened the truck door, not even attempting to hide his grin.

"Tandy? What did she want?"

Mad Dog shrugged. "She didn't say."

"She probably let the cat out. And let me guess. You thought it would force me to communicate with Mindy."

"Yep. Bye now." Mad Dog rolled down the window. "We should let Tandy know how her idea plays out."

I had no plans to give Tandy any info on my relationship.

At Mindy's back door, I whispered to Sir as I knocked. "What do you think will win out? Her dislike of me or her worry about you?"

The curtains moved. Then the door swung open. "You found him. I've been looking for him since I got home. I'm sorry if he was in your herb garden again."

"Again?" I gave the cat what I hoped was a scolding look.

"Never mind." She reached out for him. "Where was he?"

"In my den." I leaned on the frame, making it impossible for her to close the door. "I think he misses me."

"At least someone does." She gripped the door after setting him down. "Do you mind?"

"What happened, Mindy? I'm completely in the dark on this, and it's killing me."

That fire I'd seen often in the first month we'd known each other flashed in her blue eyes. "How many people did you tell? Did you wait until morning or send out a mass text as soon as I went home? You just had to make sure everyone knew I'd fallen for the likes of you." She crossed her arms, which apparently activated her forcefield.

"Tell what to whom?" I dragged my fingers through my hair, trying to make sense of what she'd said. "Now I'm really confused. I didn't tell anyone anything. At least not at first. Once you started avoiding me, I put out a few feelers, but even then, I never told anyone—not even Mad Dog— anything about kissing or cuddling. Or even cooking."

"You didn't tell anyone I fell head over heels for you simply because of a little bit of snow?"

Her words gave me the same sensation as being smacked with a snowball. Head over heels? That was reason enough to continue trying to win her back.

"I'd categorized that as a lot of snow for this area, and no. I didn't."

She rubbed her forehead. "Tandy knew."

"She knew what? And please tell me. Do you honestly think I was going to rush to call Tandy and chat about what happened? Really?" I studied Mindy's face, wishing I could read her thoughts.

"Probably not."

Instead of telling Mindy that Tandy was responsible for the cat ending up at my house, because that would only focus the conversation on the wrong thing, I asked the most important question. "What's really bothering you?"

"This isn't a roadblock you can just find a detour around." She glanced down as Sir ran for the door.

My boot stopped him.

"I need you to close the door." She picked up the cat and carried him into the living room.

I stepped inside and closed the door. Then I waited one minute, then two.

"You're still here."

"You asked me to close the door, not leave. And, for the record, I don't think you're a roadblock."

She stood on the opposite side of the kitchen. "Maybe I'm not ready."

"For?" I didn't read minds, and I needed answers.

She blew out a frustrated breath. "It was too easy for me to think you were the person I'd read about, building up your ego and leaving a string of broken hearts behind. Trust is required in a relationship."

"I agree that trust is important. Have I broken your trust?"

She shook her head, and the look in her eyes as she opened her mouth told me what was coming.

I held up a finger. "Do not give me the 'it's not you; it's me' line. I thought you enjoyed my company. We had fun cooking, right?"

"I don't want to be your next broken heart." Her lip quivered as she inched closer to the truth.

Seeing that hurt broke my heart a little more.

"I don't want that either. I don't want anyone to break your heart." If I offered a path forward, would she be willing to trust me? "What if we back it up a little? Admittedly, I rushed to kiss you, but in my defense, I'd been thinking about it. A lot. Is there any chance we can start over?" I held her gaze, hoping she could read my sincerity.

Her lips pinched, and she opened her mouth and closed it twice before finally speaking. "I need to think about it."

I could be patient. There was a saying about good things coming to those who waited. "Absolutely." This conversation had gone better than I'd hoped. While I'd learned only a little about what bothered her, she hadn't shot me down. "Would you like me to drop off dinner tonight? I was planning to make pan-seared halibut." What I didn't tell her was that I'd had it shipped from Alaska just for her. And I'd ordered it before we'd ever kissed.

"That would be nice."

"All right, well . . ." I opened the door and sighed when a gray streak swooshed between my legs. "I'll get him."

He sat at my door, tail swishing back and forth. Her cat liked me. And if I started feeding him yummy food, he'd come over more often.

That wasn't a bad thing at all.

CHAPTER 29

*J*effrey made a point of brushing his hand against mine multiple times as he handed back the cat. "I'll bring dinner by in a bit."

"Thanks." I had a lot of thinking to do while Jeffrey cooked.

Did I believe he'd told Tandy about kissing me? No. And jumping to crazy conclusions had more to do with my insecurities than with his past. The parts I guarded were still hidden away, but those hurts had more power than I wanted. More power than they deserved.

I pulled sheets of pretty stationery out of my desk and sat down at the kitchen table. With my favorite pen, I started writing.

For decades, people deepened relationships by writing letters back and forth. So, if he was willing, we'd start there. Putting words on a page was easier than baring my soul with him staring into it as I spoke.

Dear Jeffrey,

Dear sounded formal, and he'd probably assume bad news followed, but that greeting had been tested by time and worked well for opening a letter. I was definitely over-thinking this.

> *You said not to say that it was me and not you, but there isn't a truer statement to describe why I've pulled away. My initial reaction was to doubt you, but given the briefest amount of logical thought, those silly conclusions fell apart.*
>
> *My overthinking kicked in when you walked me home. I won't go into all the reasons for my insecurities in this letter, but I'm hoping you are open to letting this be how we start over.*
>
> *It's comical for neighbors to exchange letters, I suppose, but that's how it was done in the olden days—not that you'd know anything about that time period.*

One page stretched into two, and I didn't stop for fear my honesty would retreat to a safer place.

> *I loved hearing about your dreams, cooking with you. Spending time with you was a treat because there were spans of time when my enjoyment wasn't buried in a million other thoughts.*
>
> *When I spend time with my friends, my overthinking tends to calm a bit. The same is true when I'm with you.*
>
> *If letter writing is acceptable to you, I'd love a letter in return. And I'm hoping this method of communication will make me less susceptible to your charms.*

There was more I needed to tell him, but this was a beginning. My reasons for holding back weren't selfless. His reaction to this letter would inform my decisions about how much to say.

I stared at the bottom of the page, trying to decide how to close the letter.

The distinct sound of his boots on the driveway preceded his knock, and I signed the letter simply and honestly.

As I walked to the door, I tucked it into an envelope.

He held up a plate covered in foil. "For you."

Very clever of him to bring my dinner on a dish I'd feel obligated to return.

"And this is for you." I handed over the letter. "After you read it, you can let me know what you think."

"I will. And you can bring that back whenever. I have a lot of plates and rarely have company, so it's no hurry." He held up the letter. "I'll go read it now."

Was he a fast reader? Would I know what he thought before going to bed tonight? Waiting would be torturous, but I'd made him wait a week for no good reason. It had seemed like a good reason at the time, but in hindsight, it seemed more like I was provoking drama and seeking attention.

I wanted to believe all the sweet words and kisses were genuine, and that I could be someone he'd find captivating. After spending so much of my life feeling like I was outside the circle, I doubted it could be true because Jeffrey was a center-of-the-circle kind of guy.

Standing at the counter, positioned so I could see Jeffrey's front door, I ate the best halibut I'd ever tasted. He was spoiling me.

AN HOUR LATER, I gave up watch in the kitchen and started pacing through the house. If he didn't like the idea of letters, I could live with that. I wasn't exactly normal, and I needed someone who could embrace odd and quirky ideas. As time stretched on, I lectured myself. I'd stopped hoping love would find me. I'd given up having dreams and replaced them with plans, ones that made me happy. But after a taste of being in Jeffrey's arms, I hated the idea of being alone. He'd had plenty of time to respond, and he hadn't.

I channeled my disappointment, positive that no news was bad news.

Before Jeffrey, I'd done perfectly fine by myself. Not completely by myself. I had Sir Lancelot, and when he wasn't racing out my back door, he was good company. It might take time, but I'd be fine again. Eventually.

There was a rap on the window, and I ran to the kitchen. Jeffrey waved and pointed to the door. After blowing me a kiss, he strode back to his house.

Sitting on my porch was a cake carrier. Inside was one of the chocolate cakes he'd made me on Christmas, and on top was a letter.

I set the cake on the counter and cut myself a slice. Once I had a bite in my mouth, I tore open the letter, not in the prim and proper way they likely did it in the past.

Dearest Mindy,

I'll start by saying that I'm hurt you think my charm cannot be transported through my written words. I will work to prove you wrong.

Letter writing is a most agreeable pastime, and I look forward to our correspondences. Hopefully my sparkling and witty humor conveys.

Humor aside, I'm fine communicating this way. Much like me, it's charming. And I'm looking forward to getting to know you better. (That was not supposed to be read in a sultry and insinuating voice.)

I stared at a blank page a while before putting words down because it's been a long time since I've put my thoughts on paper. And I've never written letters to a woman before.

While I can be obtuse and oblivious at times, your hurt is apparent. I noticed. At first, I thought I was the reason, but that thinking puts me at the center of your world and is incredibly vain. (No response is needed here.)

If I could reach in and remove that wound, I would. But I can't. What I can do and what I plan to do is listen and sit with you as you deal with the hurt . . . if you'll let me.

Kissing you wasn't an impulse decision, made because we were stranded together. I spent all day outside because as much as I wanted to fan the obvious spark between us, I struggled to be true to myself. While drawing a line in the sand about the age of women I date may seem silly (you might understand because you suggested writing letters when we have the technology to send words through the air from one phone to another) I needed to hold to that boundary.

Changing my behavior involved a series of victories and setbacks. (Ava may have mentioned the twenty-something I invited over for steaks. Nothing happened. That was more than a year ago. Please don't hold it against me.)

Not sure why I decided to include the opposite of a resume in this letter, but getting back to my point, I liked you, and when you so angrily announced your age, I knew what I wanted.

You.

I look forward to your next letter.

Always,

Jeffrey

P.S. I'm hoping that sending treats with my letter will score me extra points. Enjoy the cake.

I cried on my slice of cake. Then I ate it. Tears were no reason to throw out such deliciousness. Fueled by chocolate and helped by Jeffrey's charms, I sat down with a pen and paper.

In this moment when I felt like I could reveal anything to him, that he was safe, I penned a second letter. This time he'd learn about my heartache and why I struggled. Feeling like a burden was awful; being betrayed had left me scarred.

Once his house was dark, I tiptoed across the driveway and taped the letter to his door.

Maybe tonight, I'd finally get a good night's sleep.

*P*erhaps being so honest wasn't the best strategy for winning her heart, but Mindy had to know what she was getting out of the deal. I was flawed and far from perfect, but my feelings for her were real.

I owed her that honesty.

Opening a restaurant had taught me loads about dedicating myself to something I loved. Mindy sparked those same emotions. What had started as attraction deepened every time I saw her vulnerable side and when she ignored my orders, thinking she'd help me.

Now through words penned on feminine floral paper, I was seeing inside her even more. It was too soon to use the word love, and caution was necessary because I'd never traveled this road before, one I'd avoided at all costs for a long time.

Now, that road called to me, but I only wanted to travel it with Mindy as a companion.

After dropping off my letter, which had been written on a sheet of paper from my printer because I didn't keep special stationery for little notes, I'd gone through the routine of getting ready for bed, then I'd sat in the dark, thinking. While I contemplated, her shadow had passed the window.

It hadn't taken long for her to deliver a return letter.

After a half hour, assuming she'd given up watching my front door, I grabbed the letter and carried it to bed.

Jeffrey,

In my early twenties, I got engaged after a whirlwind romance. At the time, I thought he was perfect. Then I started getting sick. He was sweet and tender at first. He'd text during the day to check on me.

Plans for the wedding were put on hold while I worked to uncover what was wrong with me. The celiac diagnosis came as a shock. A warm loaf of bread was my favorite comfort food back then.

Going to restaurants was more difficult because of reasons I explained before. At first my fiancé didn't complain, just moped a little. And when I told him he could go to dinner with friends without me, he did. Then dinners with friends expanded to dinners with other women. My friends would text me with reports.

I had changed, and he liked the old me.

Finally, it all ended when I saw him kissing a woman in the lobby of a hotel. He didn't know he'd been caught, but I stopped calling him. That was when I had to swallow the hard truth. I'd been holding onto him. When I didn't call or text, contact ended.

He never broke up with me. The ring is still in my drawer. (If you know of a good place to sell a diamond ring, it's probably time I do that.)

He was outgoing and popular, the life of the party. I was never that. When food allergies were heaped on, I became a burden.

That was how I felt.

But it doesn't excuse his betrayal.

In those last twenty-four hours we spent together at your house, the whirlwind frightened me.

But I'm not afraid of the whirlwind. The fear of betrayal sends my thoughts in crazy directions, but the idea that I'd hold you back, that I am a burden is what has me running for cover.

Thank you for being open about who you were and how you worked to be different. While I don't have the option of getting over my food allergies, I am working on what I say to myself.

I've never met anyone like you.

And when I tried avoiding you, you let me have my space but kept dropping off food. You didn't let go.

Thank you for that.

Hopeful,

Mindy

I slipped out of bed and scrawled out a short reply.

Dearest Mindy,

If I were prone to violence (I'm not, but I know people) I'd be asking for names and addresses. I didn't miss the fact that you omitted names from the story. Protecting the guilty says something about you. Or maybe you don't like the way his name looks written down.

As for unloading a ring, I'll look into it.

You might be the strongest person I've ever met.

Always,

Jeffrey

P.S. I can never recreate your favorite comfort food, but it won't stop me from trying.

I laid the letter on my counter, set an alarm for early in the morning, and crawled in bed. I had bread to bake before she left to work.

I'd spent hours and hours and made multiple loaves, trying to get a gluten-free loaf that didn't have the texture of sand and crumble with minimal handling. And she'd commented about how good that bread was. I'd try to make my next loaf even better.

Even before I'd given my heart permission to care, Mindy had inspired changes in me.

~

WHEN I WAS sure Mindy would be up, I set a basket with the bread, a few baked omelets, and my letter on her porch. Then acting like a preteen, I knocked and hurried away.

Instead of standing near the window and waiting to catch a glimpse of her expression, I got dressed. We hadn't been exchanging letters for even a full day, and my handwriting had gotten more practice than in the last year.

When the back door opened, I strolled into the kitchen. "Morning, Mad Dog. Know any places where I could get a good deal when selling a diamond ring?"

He rubbed his forehead. "I was expecting a different question. Selling one? When did you buy one?"

"I'm going to need ideas about that, too, but not right away." I poured him a cup of coffee. "Drink this. It might help those lines in your forehead go away."

"It's way too early for riddles. Have you patched things up or not?"

"We're patching. And—I'm only going to say this once and might deny it if you bring it up again—you were right. It's not all about me." I glanced out the window as she walked to her car. "She has an engagement ring that she desires to sell."

"But not your ring?"

My gaze stayed focused on her, and my heart thudded a bit when she looked at the window and smiled. I waved; then she climbed in and drove away. "I've never bought a ring of any sort."

"But?"

"I'm going to need advice. You've successfully proposed twice. I've never even thought to ask."

"Until now."

I pulled keys out of my pocket. "Now is too soon to ask, but I'm thinking about it now. I plan to wait until I'm absolutely sure she'll say yes."

Mad Dog laughed. "Take it from me. It's easier that way. Because if she doesn't answer immediately, those milliseconds of waiting are bad for the ticker." He set his cup in the sink and walked to the door. "Never thought I'd see the day. But Ava assured me I would. Ask Beau about selling the ring. I bet he'll have a suggestion."

"And about buying?"

"I bought mine at a warehouse store, which worked out well for me, but I do not recommend. Beau and Clint both had rings designed. Talk to them."

Leading up to Valentine's Day, I'd expected to be consumed with restaurant reviews and social media mentions. But I was toying with the idea of buying a ring, and thoughts of Mindy crowded out most of the other stuff.

And I'd never been happier.

CHAPTER 31

I tied up the stack of letters and held them to my chest. They'd been read so many times, entire paragraphs were etched in my memory. I laughed ahead of every joke and cried at several other parts.

After pulling the ribbon loose, I opened the last letter again.

Dearest Mindy,

What you wrote about dreams and plans has been rattling around in my brain. Plans are actionable. I like that about them, but in dreams, there is a whisper of hope.

I hope (see what I did there) you've been inspired to give dreams a chance again.

Since I agreed not to deliver two meals a day, I'm sending a new seafood spice mix I've been playing with. Enjoy.

Always,

Jeffrey

With every letter, I was falling in love, and I couldn't

blame it on kisses or cuddling by a fire. Bit by bit, I learned more about Jeffrey, and I shared pieces of myself.

It was strange to feel such intimacy with someone I only exchanged letters with and saw through the window. But in many ways, we were closer now than when we'd snuggled on his sofa.

But I did miss the snuggling.

With each letter, he'd sent a treat or a meal. The food was good, but his words fed my soul. I'd asked him to stop sending me a meal twice a day, and he'd acquiesced after several letters were exchanged and new terms of spoiling were agreed upon. That wasn't what he called it, but his daily food deliveries made me feel indulged in the best of ways.

Jeffrey never pushed for more than letters. He was waiting on me. After Valentine's Day, he'd have a reason to seek me out. And it was requiring all my patience to wait for that. If I saw him earlier, I might spill the surprise.

One more day. I could wait that long.

With the folder open for tomorrow's event, I scanned the information, a lot of which was blank. It was hard enough to concentrate on work, knowing Donna would be spotlighting Jeffrey's restaurant tomorrow night. She'd already been posting teasers about where she was headed without giving enough details for people to figure it out. But even though she and her husband were staying not far away at an adorable and very private cabin, we hadn't gotten together for a visit. My relationship with Jeffrey had not been discussed, with her or with anyone.

I blinked, focusing my thoughts on work. Tomorrow night, I'd be busy with this event, which meant I wouldn't be staring at my phone and waiting for Jeffrey to find out what I'd done.

Lilith waved as she walked past my door. "Morning."

"Have a sec?"

She stepped into my office. "Sure. What's up?"

I turned the folder so she could see the page. "I wanted to ask about the event tomorrow."

She glanced at the page, then met my gaze. "When I laid this on your desk, I'd forgotten you had secret reservations at the restaurant."

"You didn't tell anyone about that, did you? Or cancel them, right? They aren't for me, but someone is going to have dinner there tomorrow night."

"I didn't cancel. Do I need to change the name on the reservation?"

"Could you just let them know it won't be you?"

Lines crinkled near her eyes. "Not sure what's up with all the secrecy, but I'm looking forward to finding out."

"It's good. I promise. Anyway . . ." I tapped the folder. "There is a lot of information missing. And what's here is vague. When I pull up the file in the system, it's the same way. You booked this, right?"

"Yep." She pointed at the name. "The man asked not to be identified in the paperwork. He's not like a mob boss or anything. He's just being discreet."

"Excessively so."

She grinned. "It's a surprise for his girlfriend. Dinner. Dancing. All the romance. He'll meet you in the main gathering room at the time listed in the file."

I only had pieces of answers. "What about food? The caterer isn't filled in."

"Oh! That's my mistake." She picked up a pen and wrote on the page. "He's providing his own food."

"We allow that?" All the events here had been catered by a vendor on our list.

"Special case. And did you see the note about black tie? I'd like for you to wear an evening gown. I should've mentioned it earlier. I'm sorry. If you don't have anything suitable, I'm happy to suggest some places." She pulled bills out of her wallet. Several. And they weren't ones. "The client wanted to cover the extra expense."

I hesitated before taking the cash. Nothing in my closet was suitable for black tie. I'd managed lots of events, but before working here, most of them were business-type functions, and none of those required this level of dressy.

"Thank you."

She pointed at the door. "Tomorrow night should be easy. The man has everything handled, but I need a coordinator here. I hope you don't mind. Beau already made plans."

"It's fine. Enjoy Valentine's Day with your husband."

"I appreciate that. My husband spoils me. My first husband wasn't anything like that, and I doubted guys like Beau existed. He proved me wrong. Dream guys do exist." She waved a hand. "Anyway, I'll text you the name of a few places. Go shopping."

"I will."

After pointing at the door, she shooed me out. "I meant now."

"Yes, ma'am." I shut off my computer, closed the folder on the mystery event, and walked out to the car. When names of boutiques popped up in my messages, I figured out where they were and headed that way.

While I loved the idea of buying an evening gown, wearing one for someone else's romantic celebration tasted bittersweet.

THE THIRD BOUTIQUE had several options I loved. The hard part now was deciding.

Winter had ended its stay in Texas, and spring weather kept the temperature near perfect most days. I wouldn't have to wear my red coat over an evening gown, thank goodness.

The salesperson smiled as she walked over. "Having trouble deciding?"

"Yes. I'm working an event, and an evening gown is required."

"So you are wanting something elegant and professional."

"But I want to be able to wear it for other events in the future." Even dreaming I'd have a reason to wear an evening gown in the future was a sign of how much my thought processes had changed.

"Mind if I see them on you?" She pointed at the dressing room.

"Sure." Closed into the room, I changed out of my slacks and blouse and slipped into an emerald-green A-line dress with capped sleeves.

While it was elegant, it didn't strike the right note, but I'd get the saleswoman's opinion. I stepped out, and her noncommittal smile confirmed my thoughts.

"This is pretty, but let's see the next one."

The next one was a black sparkly sheath dress. It showed off my figure more than the last gown. I felt pretty good as I glided out of the changing room.

"Wow. This fits you so well. You're stunning. I think we have a winner, but you should try on that last one."

After stepping into the last dress, I stared into the mirror. This was the one. The vibrant blue halter dress reminded me of my turtlenecks, but this gown didn't have sleeves. It hugged my subtle curves and had a slit up to my thigh.

In this dress, I felt confident and beautiful.

The saleslady touched a hand to her heart as I walked out of the changing room. "Wear that, and you'll own the place. This is absolutely the one."

"I agree."

After buying the gown, I made one last stop. Lilith had also sent the name of a lingerie shop, and for that dress to have maximum impact, which I wanted purely for my own enjoyment, I needed particular foundation pieces.

A woman smiled as the bell jingled above the door. "Hello, how may I help you?"

I described the dress and explained what I needed.

"Right this way. I'm Delaney." She extended her hand.

"Mindy."

"You work at the venue, right? With Lilith?"

"I do." I hadn't spent a lot of time in town, but it was clear that, out here, degrees of separation rarely exceeded two and that news traveled at lightning speed.

She leaned closer as if sharing a secret. "My best friend just married Beau's son. Such a great family."

"How nice. I didn't know they were dating." Lilith had mentioned Tessa and Garrett on the day I was late, and back in early December, they'd only been friends.

"They didn't date long. I'm not sure what it is about this town—and that ranch in particular—but love and romance have spread like wildfire. Even a handful of the ranch hands have found someone special." She tapped a rack and studied me before holding up a bra. "This one should work."

After trying it on under my new dress and confirming it was absolutely what I needed, I paid with the remainder of what Lilith had given me. "Thank you so much."

"You're very welcome. I hope tomorrow evening is spectacular."

I nodded my appreciation but didn't stop to explain that I'd be working. This dress would be seen by just two people, and based on the few details in the file, they only had eyes for each other.

But I loved the idea of getting dressed up just the same.

I drove home, excited about tomorrow. I hadn't spent this

much time focused on how I looked in a long time. It felt good. And I wouldn't be getting all dolled up to impress Jeffrey because the restaurant would be extra busy on the special day.

With the garment bag hung over my shoulder, I walked toward the house. Lilith had given me the rest of the day off, so I'd take time to do my nails. Maybe even my toenails.

What sort of wild woman was I becoming?

CHAPTER 32

JEFFREY

*W*hat sort of dress had Mindy bought for tomorrow night? It hung over her shoulder, hidden by that black bag. Before stepping inside, she glanced at my window.

I lifted my mug, and she grinned.

Old-fashioned as it might be, letter-writing had cultivated a deeper relationship between us. When she doubted me or even herself, she could read over what I'd written, and each time she did, the words solidified a bit more as truth. At least that was how it had been with me.

While I wasn't ready to propose—waiting wasn't always a bad thing—I had taken a bit of Mad Dog's advice. There was no doubt Mindy would be excited when she saw me standing in the gathering room tomorrow night.

My tux was pressed and ready, and all the ingredients for an amazing dinner had been acquired.

But I didn't want her spending all day thinking I hadn't singled her out on Valentine's, so I formed a plan. And ordered a dozen roses.

~

AFTER WEEKS of sending letters back and forth, I was eager to talk to her. Even when Sir snuck out, I'd had Mad Dog take him over so I didn't break the magical spell. Waiting for our next face-to-face conversation had stirred anticipation. I figured a surprise meeting—for her, not for me—would be fun. Then she'd never suspect I was the discreet client.

Early Valentine's morning, I carried the rose bushes Stephanie had given me over to the garden and set the vase of long-stem roses on the porch. Now that the threat of frost was over, I could get these plants in the ground, and the best place for them was right by Mindy's bedroom window.

After clearing away leaves and debris, I dug two holes. Whistling as I stuck the plants in the ground and mounded the dirt around the base, I waited for Mindy to make an appearance.

It would be a while before these bushes had blooms on them, but they'd be beautiful. I'd have to let Mindy know she was free to cut some to make bouquets if she wanted. Today, the roses I'd ordered would have to suffice.

The front door swung open, and she stepped out in her bare feet. Polish the color of a blazing sunset covered her toenails, and her fingernails matched. "What are you doing?" Amused crinkles near her eyes betrayed the curt question.

"Planting roses."

"Why?" She threaded her fingers through her hair, then patted it down.

I stood and crossed my arms as a reminder not to hug her. There'd be time for that later. "Roses do better in the ground than in pots. At least for me."

She treated me to an eye roll. "I meant, why now?"

"Two reasons. I knew you were home. And it's Valentine's

Day." I pointed to the arrangement I'd strategically placed where she wouldn't notice it when she walked out.

Her mouth fell open. "Jeffrey."

"And I was whistling to make sure you'd know I was out here by your window."

Smiling, she swallowed, then walked down the steps toward me.

"I'm covered in dirt." I held my hands up as proof. This was the part I hadn't thought through well.

"I don't care." Her arms wrapped around my neck, and her cheek pressed to mine. "I've missed hugging you. And you don't have to keep your hands out to the sides. I plan to shower before leaving for work."

After giving my hands a good shake, I held her. "I've missed this too."

"Tonight will be busy at the restaurant, I'm guessing."

"Booked solid. How about you? Have big plans?" I pulled back only far enough to look her in the eye.

"Work. Some guy booked the venue to surprise his girl-friend. I'll be there to make sure everything goes smoothly."

"Intriguing." I kept my expression neutral, trying not to give her any spoilers or reasons to be suspicious.

"Very. And it's black tie, so I'll be in an evening gown. I've never worked a function in a tight floor-length dress, so it's sure to be interesting."

I kissed her forehead, letting my eyes close as I imagined how amazing she'd look in her pretty new dress. "I hope it goes well."

"And I'm wishing you lots of happy customers tonight." Her lips pinched, and she buried her face in the curve of my neck.

Mindy had a secret. Her lying skills weren't on par with mine, not something I was proud of, but she'd hidden her face and used cuddling as a means to do it. But it didn't make the feel of her breath on my neck any less stimulating.

I let my lips skim her ear. "Go shower. I don't want to make you late for work."

She pressed a kiss to my neck. "Thank you for the roses."

"You're welcome. Before you go, I have another question."

Her eyebrows lifted, silently inviting me to ask.

"Would you go on a date with me?" I'd laughed at Mad Dog when he'd done everything in reverse romance-wise, and then when it was my turn, I hadn't done much better.

"I'd like that. A lot. You did say we'd go dancing." She let her hands slide down my chest. "Call me or knock on my door."

"I will."

She bent to pick up the roses, her pajama pants clinging to her legs in all the right spots. The back of her tank top was covered in dirt in all the places I'd had my hands.

"You're beautiful in the morning."

Her cheeks flushed, making them only a shade lighter than the roses. She wiggled her fingers in a wave, then closed the door.

Tonight seemed like a lifetime away.

CHAPTER 33

MINDY

Since I'd be working late, I lingered at home longer than I normally would.

With a bag of trash in one hand, I yanked open the door. And Sir took full advantage. He was giving me the impression he didn't want to live with me anymore. After dropping the bag in the bin, I walked around to the herb garden.

He wasn't there, and the dirt hadn't been disturbed.

Where was that stupid cat?

"Morning? Looking for your little Houdini?" Mad Dog set his cowboy hat on his head, that warm smile spread across his face.

"I am. Have you seen him?"

He hooked a thumb toward the door. "Ran in when I had the door open. It's not locked."

"I'm sorry he's such a bother."

"Not a big deal. Jeffrey doesn't seem to mind either, though I dare say, he wouldn't be disappointed to find you with the cat in his house. Cat optional."

I blinked, processing his words. "Um, okay."

He laughed. "Just saying."

"Maybe someday." My answer surprised even me.

Mad Dog's grin widened. "Have a great day!"

"You too." I pushed open Jeffrey's door, feeling a little like a stalker creeping around his place while he wasn't home. "Sir, where are you? Please do not leave a mess in this man's house."

More than once, Sir had spent a chunk of the day here because I hadn't noticed him slipping out. My worst fear was he'd find something like Jeffrey's laundry to use as a litter box. Searching, I walked into the kitchen.

Sir Lancelot jumped off the counter and dashed out of the room.

"Wait! Hey!" I glanced at the spot he'd vacated and stopped.

The same brand of cat food and cat treats I kept on hand were sitting on the counter. And one of the treat bags had teeth marks in it, but it didn't look like Sir had been successful in getting it open.

The search was on again. I checked the living room, the den, even Jeffrey's office. I walked down the hallway, skipping rooms where the door was closed. Surely Sir hadn't become that conniving.

I wandered through a guest room that shared a full bath with another room. Tucked in a corner of the bathroom was a litter box. Jeffrey probably worried Sir would leave him a surprise, and not a good one.

I'd found a litter box, but no cat. And I'd looked in every room but one. Going into Jeffrey's room felt like a horrible invasion of privacy. The door was open a few inches, and I peeked in without opening it farther. Sir lay sprawled in the middle of the bed.

"I've about had it with you, Sir. Get over here."

His tail flipped, slapping the mattress, but no other part of him moved.

"Please don't make me come get you."

Another flip of the tail. I knew that was kitty sign language for a bad word. While I was pondering what to do, my phone rang. And as soon as I saw who was calling, I swiped to answer.

"Donna, hi!"

"You home? I wanted to spend at least a few minutes with you while I'm in town."

"I'll be home in two minutes." I pointed at the cat when he turned his head to look at me. "Come on over."

"Yay! You can give me the dirt on the Cowboy Chef." She let loose her contagious laugh.

"The only dirt on that cowboy is from his rose garden. You can see it when you come over."

"Wait. Am I going to his house or your house? I need more details. All. The. Details."

It was my turn to laugh. "I'll explain when you get here. I'm texting over directions." I stuck the phone in my pocket and marched into Jeffrey's room. After a brief pause to inhale his masculine scent, I scooped up my cat. "Are you trying to cause trouble?"

Before walking out, I surveyed the room. There were no clothes on the floor, and it was generally clutter free. The bed had the comforter pulled up, but he hadn't exactly made the bed.

When I spotted the stack of letters on his nightstand, I sighed against Sir's fur. "He kept all my letters."

Sir's tail flipped again.

I carried my escape artist back home and tossed him into my bedroom. That way I wouldn't have to repeat my search for him after opening the door for Donna.

≈

WHEN I OPENED MY DOOR, Donna was facing Jeffrey's house. "This is cozy."

"I needed a place to live, and he wasn't using this house. He's my landlord." I didn't want to tell Donna all the stuff I'd normally share with my friend because she might think I was trying to influence her.

Donna shook her head as she stepped inside. "I've known you a long time, Mindy. The look on your face is not there because he's a good landlord." Her gaze landed on the roses, and she wrapped me in a hug. "Oh, Mindy, this is wonderful. Tell me all about him."

"This wasn't a thing when I spoke to you about him at Christmas. I didn't plan on saying anything today because I want you to judge his food on the merits. He's a fabulous cook. Not just steaks and potatoes either. Don't get me wrong. People rave about his steaks, but even the food he's made for me with all my food restrictions makes my mouth water just thinking about it." I pulled out a chair, then sat in the one beside it. "I really like him." Admitting it to someone other than myself and Jeffrey made me smile. This was real. And I could trust him not to walk away.

"Is he older, younger? Tall? Short?" She leaned forward, her chin resting on her stacked hands.

"I know you've looked him up."

She'd looked him up the same day I'd mentioned him.

"Is he as hot as the pictures?"

"Every bit as much." I sniffed the roses. "But the stuff about how he's a heartbreaker—that's not true. At least not anymore."

She stared at the roses. "I read those write-ups. But I know you, and apart from the one we don't mention, you haven't picked any bad ones."

"Donna, I haven't seriously dated anyone since I ended

things with my ex, if you consider how the relationship faded away ending things."

"My point exactly. You wouldn't have waited this long to fall for a heartbreaker. You know what you want, and it sounds like you've found it. I'm really happy for you."

"One other thing."

She tapped her nails on the table. "Oooh, a secret?"

Just from the way I said something, she knew what was coming.

"He doesn't know we're friends or that I suggested his restaurant to you."

She bounced in her seat. "Please let me tell him. And Denise and Debra too."

"Sure. But right now, Jeffrey and I are only at the roses and a date stage. So don't make it sound like we're nearly engaged or anything. Please."

"Of course." She tapped away on her phone. "But you will be. And I can't wait to see your happy face walking down the aisle."

I didn't need my friend getting my hopes up, but Jeffrey's surprise this morning and every letter he'd sent made me want a happily-ever-after with him.

STILL IN MY ROBE, I peeked around the curtains before opening the door. I'd worked for a few hours, then rushed home to get dressed for tonight.

"Stephanie, come on in. I had to make sure it was you."

"Show me your dress. It sounds amazing based on your description. Too bad Jeffrey is busy at the restaurant. He won't be here to see you leaving for the event."

My cheeks heated. "Maybe I'll have an occasion to wear it again some time."

"We can always create an occasion. Wouldn't a black-tie cocktail hour at the winery be fun? I'll be launching a new wine next year."

"That would be a wonderful way to launch it."

She pulled her dark hair over her shoulder. "It's been a long time since I've been really excited about something."

"I'm happy to help you plan the event. Lilith won't mind if I freelance a bit."

"Thanks. I'm glad we connected. I needed a friend."

I wasn't in the habit of hugging people when I was wearing a robe, but that didn't stop me from launching myself at Stephanie. "Me too."

I loved my college friends, and hanging out with Lilith and her crew was always entertaining, but Stephanie and I had clicked in a different way.

Laughing, she wiped her eyes. "All right. Show me that dress."

I took a few steps down the hall, then stopped. "I'm crazy about your brother." After telling her what probably wasn't a secret to anyone, I turned and marched down the hall.

"He's crazy about you, too, Mindy." She stepped into my room and covered her mouth as she stared at the dress hanging on my closet door. After several heartbeats, she nodded. "It's lovely. Simply perfect."

"Thank you. I know there's no chance of Jeffrey seeing me in it, but I really wish he could."

"Me too." She grinned. "He'd lose his mind."

I just wanted him to lose his heart . . . to me.

CHAPTER 34

*A*fter changing into my tuxedo at Stephanie's house, I drove to the venue. Mindy's car was parked in the same spot she used every day. I tucked a letter under her wiper blade, knowing she wouldn't find it until much later.

I gave my collar a quick tug as I strolled to our meeting place. It was a few minutes before the time I'd told Lilith, but I guessed Mindy was already there, so I opted to use the side entrance.

The door creaked as I walked into the dimly lit space. In the middle of the room, a single table was covered with a white linen tablecloth and set with two place settings. Roses that matched her nails were in an arrangement in the center.

Mindy turned to face me. I'd never mentioned anything to her about my feelings about her turtlenecks, but she was wearing a dress that had all the wonderful features of them except with a bonus. The evening gown showed off her shoulders. I allowed myself a sweeping look, not lingering too long on how it framed her perfect silhouette.

"You look . . . that dress . . . wow." Trying to complete a sentence was hopeless at the moment.

Panic etched her face, and she shook her head. "No. You shouldn't be here."

This wasn't the reaction I'd expected. I stepped closer, extending my hand. "Surprise."

"Jeffrey, it's Valentine's Day." She didn't resist when I slipped my arms around her.

"That's sort of the point, Mindy. Valentine's Day is all about romance and flowers. And chocolate. I have that covered as well."

"Listen to me. You have to go to the restaurant. Now. Don't ask any questions. Just go." She pushed off my chest, and her gaze glided down, then back up. "For me."

"I'll go *for you*, but I need to stop and change."

"Don't. You're perfect." She looked up after she said it, her gaze meeting mine. "For me."

Whatever was waiting for me at the restaurant wouldn't mind a few extra minutes. I pulled Mindy into my arms and kissed her like my future depended on it.

I was quite sure it did.

She tugged out of my arms and pushed me toward the door. "Call me later."

"It might be late."

Her lips brushed my cheek. "No matter what time."

I SLIPPED in the back door, curious about why it was imperative I showed up at the restaurant tonight. I'd spent hours in the kitchen, making sure every last detail was perfect before leaving to meet Mindy. It was an important night, but surprising Mindy had been a higher priority.

Laurel hurried toward me. "Oh my gosh, I'm so happy to see you., I hope this doesn't mean your night blew up, but we can talk about that later. In my schedule, Lilith had reserved your table tonight."

"Okay?" It was taking Laurel longer than necessary to get to the point.

"Lilith isn't here. And you'd left strict orders not to be bothered tonight. For future reference, using all caps isn't necessary."

Laurel had been my assistant since the day we'd opened, and there was no one better suited to working with me, but there were times when she shredded my patience. This was one of those times.

"So we have an empty table? That doesn't seem like a problem."

Her head wagged back and forth. "I know you keep up with influencers. I've seen you scrolling on your phone. Anyway Donna, of Donna Talks Food, is at your table, With her husband. All week, she's been dropping teasers about what restaurant she selected as her Valentine's Day destination. She never mentioned this place, but after the things she wrote, I'd want to eat here."

"What's that supposed to mean?"

She waved, as if swiping the words out of the way. "Have you been reading her stuff?"

"Not this week. I saw a post about it a week back. My mind has been on other things."

"I don't think Mindy wants to be called a thing."

"Since when are y'all on a first name basis?"

"I delivered her food every night, remember?" She straightened my bow tie. "You look fab. I'm sure she was impressed. Now, go."

Even a month ago, I would've been over the moon about someone with such reach showing up here, but right now, I had to convince myself this was worth leaving Mindy.

After two steps, I spun around, and Laurel bumped into me.

She huffed. "Your table is that way."

"Have you talked to Mindy tonight?"

Laurel put her hands together in front of her lips. "Okay, I get that you want to talk about Mindy *all the time*, but you need to scoot your bootie out to that table. Now."

"Answer the question."

"No. I haven't spoken to her since the last time I dropped off food."

How did Mindy know the Donna woman was here? Maybe Lilith had set this up and mentioned it to Mindy.

Still trying to fit the pieces together, I strode into my private nook. "Good evening."

The woman, who I assumed was Donna, gasped. "Mindy didn't exaggerate a bit. Dang."

Her husband cut her a look, then laughed. "Toby. Nice to meet you."

"Jeffrey Carpenter. Thank you for choosing to dine here tonight. I take it you know Mindy."

"I've known her a long time." Donna grinned. "We went to college together."

We chatted several minutes about how Mindy had set this in motion at Christmas, and then I shared the night's specials with them.

After posing for a selfie with Donna and her husband, I strolled out of the nook, hoping to find Laurel.

She was waiting in the hall. "How'd it go?"

"Fine. Need me for anything else?"

"You're *leaving*?"

"I have someplace to be. More accurately, I have someone to be with. Call if you need me."

"You aren't going to wait to see what Donna thinks of the food?"

"I can't charm my way into a good review. Either she likes the food, or she doesn't. My charms are needed elsewhere."

THE VENUE WAS DARK, and Mindy's car wasn't in the lot, so I raced home, parked beside her car, and knocked on her door.

Sir meowed inside, but Mindy didn't answer.

I needed to find her, but searching would be easier if I changed out of this monkey suit. I ran across the driveway, and the letter taped to my door stopped me.

I'd left a simple, heartfelt note on her car. Three words that summed up my feelings. Opening what I assumed was her response, I held my breath.

I love you too.

I threw open my front door, eager to start my search.

Mindy stood in my living room, still wearing her gown. She crossed her arms, then uncrossed them. "I got your note."

Holding up her letter, I strode toward her. "And I read yours."

She stopped my forward motion by putting her hands on my chest. "I didn't expect you until later. Did everything go okay?"

"I met Donna. She and her husband were ordering when I left."

"You didn't stay?" Her hands stayed put, but her feet inched toward me.

I dipped my head so my lips were by her ear. "Being with you was more important. Seeing you in that dress is a bonus."

Her lips skimmed my clean-shaven cheek. "You paid for it."

"Worth every penny." I stepped back to look at her dress again. "You're beautiful at night too."

"Thank you."

"The surprise at the venue tonight was so our first date would be memorable. I'm sorry it didn't work out as planned, but I love that you sent Donna to my restaurant."

"You were kind and helpful even when I wasn't. Making sure you were noticed for your talents seemed the best way to repay your kindness."

I pulled her close. "I remember seeing Clint smile at Joji and hearing the way Mad Dog talked about Ava. Now I understand how they felt. From the moment you shouted at me from the tree, flirting with you seemed as natural as breathing, so I spent a lot of time holding my breath. You dominated my thoughts even when my ego was bruised. When you hugged me after meeting Chuck the first time, my attraction went through the roof." I dotted kisses down her cheek. "And when you walked inside the fence to distract Chuck from the drunks, I felt something I'd never felt before."

She blinked, her lashes damp with tears.

"Loving you is a dream come true for me. Having you love me is even better." I brushed my lips on hers. "I love you so much I wrote it down so you'd never forget."

She cradled my face and brushed her lips on mine. "And I love you, Jeffrey Carpenter. You're just as charming on paper as you are in person, and it was worth waiting a long time for you."

I crushed her to me, capturing her mouth with mine.

After a delightfully long and passionate kiss, she patted my lapel. "The food you'd taken to the venue is in your kitchen. Were you planning to cook there?"

"I was, but now, I'll cook here."

She shook her head. "Not now. Later." She clasped my

hand and led me through the house. "Mad Dog sent over a couple of the ranch hands, two who didn't have plans tonight. Dallas and Archer helped me move the furniture in the den so we could dance."

I slipped my phone out, and after a few taps, music wafted through the room. "Dancing. This might be the most memorable first date ever."

"Thank you for surprising me at the venue. When you walked in . . ." A smile spread across her face as she slipped her hand in mine. "I loved everything about it except that you were supposed to be somewhere else."

She followed my lead, and as our feet moved across the tile floor, our lips danced.

"But now I'm here." Tonight had turned out more perfectly than I'd dared to dream.

But holding Mindy in my arms, I was sure of one thing. Some dreams did come true.

CHAPTER 35

I checked a few more items off my to-do list, eager to get home. Whatever was left could wait until tomorrow. Dinner was at Jeffrey's tonight, and he'd been dropping teases all week about making something new.

We'd been dating for weeks, and not a day had passed without the two of us spending at least a few moments together.

As I cleaned up my desk, Tandy strolled in. "Am I still on the naughty list?"

"Tandy, I'm not the least bit mad at you. But it seems to me you'll always be on the naughty list."

Her head tilted back, and she let loose a belly laugh. "You are right about that. I'm nice at home, but there's no one there to tease."

I pulled my purse out of the bottom drawer. "When you asked about the kisses, how did you know?"

"I guessed, but it was an educated guess. I've seen Jeffrey, and I've seen Jeffrey see you. Trapped together, there was no possible way y'all fought off that attraction." She danced her eyebrows. "How's it going?"

"We're happy."

"This is a book-research question. What do you love more —the small but consistent displays of affection or the grand gestures?" Tandy grinned, stirring doubt that her question had anything to do with book research.

"I don't know. I'm a bit spoiled in that regard. Jeffrey does both."

She fanned her face, then pressed a hand to her heart. "Now I can go write. Thank you for the *stimulating* conversation."

"Tandy!"

She waved over her shoulder as she walked out, proud of the fact she could make everything sound racy. I did wonder about her though. She showed up at the venue even on days she wasn't scheduled to work, which made me think she was lonely. And while she loved asking others about their love lives, she never discussed hers. That woman had a story.

Hurrying out the door, I called Stephanie after starting the engine. "I only have two minutes. I'm driving home."

"If you are calling with the hopes that I'll tell you what he's making tonight, don't bother asking. He hasn't told me either."

"Dang it."

She laughed. "But when he was by here earlier, he looked pleased as pie. When my brother dedicates himself to something, he gives it everything. He's going to make Clint look like a cold-hearted miser."

Beau doted on Lilith, and Mad Dog was more than attentive to Ava, but the entire country knew Clint Jackson was head over heels in love with Joji. With a minimal number of words, he made his love loud and clear.

But my Jeffrey outdid them all.

"Are you there?" Stephanie's voice yanked me out of my thoughts.

"I'm fine. Just sitting here in my driveway, smiling like dork."

"He loves you."

"I know. And on days I wake up thinking this is all a dream, I pull his note out from under my pillow. I'll talk to you later." I shut off the engine and hurried inside to change.

Blocking any possible escape, I held my foot in front of the door as I opened it, but my cat didn't come running. "Sir, I'm home. I'm leaving for Jeffrey's soon if you want to go."

I was a forty-two-year-old woman who spoke to her cat like he was a child, and I had the most amazing boyfriend. Not all stereotypes were accurate.

After shedding my work clothes, I stared into my closet. In the evenings, I often wore jeans or leggings, but the weather had warmed quite a bit, so I pulled shorts out of my dresser and paired them with a cute top.

Jeffrey and I had dinner together as often as our schedules allowed. And when schedules were busy, he'd come by in the morning for breakfast and a kiss. He provided the breakfast. We shared the kiss.

I skipped shoes altogether and opened the door. Before I could call Sir, he darted out and ran across the driveway.

Jeffrey must've been keeping an eye on my place because he opened his door as I approached. Then he stepped aside to let Sir zoom in. "Bought you some new treats, Sir. Didn't want you to feel left out."

"I called your sister on my way home."

He tipped his head and kissed me like he hadn't seen me in weeks even though we'd had breakfast together. "I didn't tell her what I was making."

"I know that now." I patted his chest, the firmness under his shirt reminding me that I'd wanted to ask him a question. "Did you skip just your swim or the entire workout this morning?"

"Skipped everything. Why? Can you feel flab already?" He motioned toward the kitchen. "Mind setting the table?"

"Sure." I stretched up to get plates off the top shelf. When had he moved them up here? "I want you working out so you can stay healthy and live a very long time."

Arms wrapped around me. "Are you calling me old?"

"You've aged well." My shoulders lifted involuntarily as he nuzzled my neck. "Very well."

He pressed a kiss to the sensitive spot below my ear. "I like your outfit. Haven't seen you in shorts before. I'm liking this warmer weather."

"Soon it'll be warm enough for me to swim." I didn't have his cold tolerance.

"My pool is heated."

Why didn't I know that already? "Oh?"

"I know what we're doing after dinner." He patted the side of my bare leg. "You're in for a treat."

I set plates and silverware on the table. "I've seen you in a swimsuit lots of times. Or have you not noticed me standing at the window with the curtains wide open?"

"It was more entertaining when you peeked around the curtains. But I meant dinner." He turned off the oven timer and slid a pan out of the oven. "We're having king salmon, also known as chinook salmon, that I had shipped in from Alaska. Just for you."

"Jeffrey Carpenter, where have you been all my life?" I kissed him before dropping into my chair.

He grinned, those green eyes sparkling. "I'm here now."

CUDDLED ON THE SOFA, I read, and Jeffrey was stretched out with his head in my lap. He had the font size turned way up on his reading app, but I chose not to tease him about it.

Toying with his thick, dark hair, I tried focusing on my book.

He tilted his head back to look at me. "Is that one of Tandy's?"

"No. This is the one that ended up tucked in your couch. The one I couldn't find for a while."

His chuckle gave me hot flashes.

"I wonder how it ended up there." Desire shaped his expression.

"Have you heard back from the architect?"

He tapped his phone screen and opened his email. "Let me check. I've only looked about a hundred times today." Sitting up, he grinned. "Got the plans. He made all the updates I wanted. We'll meet face-to-face in a few days."

His kiss caught me off guard, but it didn't take long for me to melt into it.

"What was that for?"

"The expansion is happening earlier than I'd hoped because of you. Because Donna sang my praises. Before, my weekends were always booked, but the weekdays were hit or miss. I couldn't risk expanding until I knew I could fill the place consistently."

"And now, it's nearly impossible to get a table without a reservation. Every night."

"You didn't even like me when you set it up, and that makes me love you more." He brushed a thumb down my cheek. "I have a meeting with a contractor in a few days. When I was in the hardware store the other day, Sutton mentioned Matthew Gallagher—not sure if you've met him. He's a local. But he used to do contracting full time. Now he does the occasional job, and I think he'll oversee the expansion. And he knows a good carpenter who can do the work." Excitement oozed off him.

"I'm so happy for you."

As he leaned in to kiss me again, Sir Lancelot jumped into my lap.

"I think someone is ready to go home. But he can wait a few minutes." After putting the cat on the floor, Jeffrey cupped my face and finished what he'd started.

Several minutes later when Sir jumped up again, Jeffrey laughed and scooped up the cat, then extended a hand to me. "I'll walk you home."

I was looking forward to the day when this was home.

CHAPTER 36

*J*knocked on Mindy's door, nervous for the first time in ages. We'd been dating for months, and I was more in love now than when I'd danced with her in my den.

"Coming." Her voice sounded far away.

Bumping my foot against my ankle, I confirmed the small box was still tucked in the sock. As much as we hugged and kissed, she'd notice if I had a ring-sized box in my pocket.

The door opened, and in a flash, her arms were around my neck. This wasn't her typically greeting, but I wasn't about to complain.

"Hello to you too." I pulled her close and enjoyed holding her.

Since we were standing here with the door open, the cat was probably halfway to Austin, but we'd hunt for him later.

When she pulled back, she wiped her cheeks. "Hi."

"Why the tears?" I ran my hand down her arm, already missing the closeness.

"PMS? Onions? Who knows?" She smiled. "Come on in."

"Are you sure everything's okay?"

"I don't have a good reason for them. I'm just happy. I leave a note on a door, and this handsome man shows up. It's like I'm living in one of Tandy's novels except you have a shirt on."

"The note did say that there would be dinner. And I can take my shirt off if you'd like."

She swatted my hands as I reached for my buttons. "Food's almost ready."

"Should I go find Sir? I'm guessing he made an escape."

"I locked him in my room, but you can let him out while I plate the food." She opened the cabinet and pulled glasses off the top shelf.

The slight stretch showed off her tall frame and lean figure. And she was wearing a turtleneck. In July?

As much as I loved seeing her lounging by my pool in a swimsuit, these figure-hugging shirts that perfectly accentuated her subtle feminine curves were still my favorite.

Instead of letting Sir out of his confinement, I stared. Unapologetically.

"Something interesting?" She didn't turn around, but her face didn't need to be visible to understand the tease.

"How many turtlenecks do you own?"

Laughter preceded her question. "Did you just ask me about turtlenecks?"

"I did. The day after your wardrobe malfunction, you wore a blue one. Those highlight you well."

A blush crept up from under the collar of this red one I hadn't seen before.

I stepped up beside her. "I like them. A lot."

"Oh please. I already like you. You don't have to feed me lines."

"Not a line. But it seems an odd clothing choice for July."

"Lilith keeps it so cold in the office. Because of hot

flashes, I guess. I dress warm and usually change when I get home, but I was in a hurry to cook."

"If you get warm, I don't mind if you change, but I do love those turtlenecks."

Her laugh rang out as I strolled down the hall to where Sir was yowling to be freed.

When I opened the door, he wound his way between my legs. "She's trying to keep you safe, you know. Some of the wild animals around here eat cats like you. And we'd all be sad if that happened."

I washed my hands before pulling out a chair for Mindy. "Smells good."

"I hope you like it." She watched as I picked up my fork.

Missing from the plate was any form of meat or seafood. That explained the tears. She was nervous about dinner, worried I wouldn't like it.

"If you don't like it, my feelings won't be hurt, and if you're hungry again in an hour, we can get you something else."

"Something more caveman-like?" I clasped her hand and pulled it to my lips. "I'm sure it's delicious."

And it was. I ate everything on my plate and had seconds before pushing back from the table.

"Seems like you enjoyed it." She slipped her hand in mine.

"I did. I might have to consider adding a vegetarian dish to the menu."

"Some people would appreciate that."

I brushed my thumb across the back of her hand. "Dessert is at my place, but first let's go look at the lights they put up at the venue." I stood and held out my hand.

"I saw the guys putting them up, but I haven't seen them on. The Christmas in July event might be the biggest one yet at the venue." She snuggled closer as we stepped outside.

It was as if she were made in the exact proportions to fit

perfectly against me. I opened the door and helped her into the truck.

As I walked around to my side, I adjusted my pant leg. Not wearing my boots felt foreign, but it would be worth it.

When we pulled into the gate, she leaned forward. "This looks amazing. People are going to love it." Her gaze settled on one of the trees, the place I'd first met her. Did she remember?

I parked and didn't have time to get out before she was headed straight for the tree where the lights were bunched together in funny ways. Conveniently, the lucky ladder was waiting at the base of the tree.

I'd only had to ask Ava nicely, and she told me where to find it.

"They must not have finished. These strands need to be readjusted." Mindy stopped at the base of the tree. "I'm going to shift these around. Will you tell me when it looks good?"

I stood behind her as she climbed up the first few rungs of the ladder. "Need help getting down? I can catch you."

She froze halfway up.

I knelt where she could see me and slipped the ring box out of my sock. "Mindy Lawrence, you've challenged me. You've inspired me. But most of all, you've made me feel loved in ways I never imagined possible. I don't want to live across the driveway from you. I want to live with you. I want you in my life, in my arms, and in my bed. Will you marry me?"

Her head bobbed up and down as tears streamed down her face.

I put one hand on the ladder. "Don't fall."

Nodding, she let go of the ladder to wipe her eyes and wobbled. I jumped up and caught her as she tipped.

She gripped my shirt. "Yes. I'll marry you."

"You can have whatever you want—a small ceremony on

the ranch, an exotic destination wedding, or we'll host the biggest wedding this county has ever seen. I want the whole world to know how I feel about you, but more than that, I want you. I love you."

Hugging me, she pressed her cheek to mine. "I love you so much."

I'd never tire of hearing those words.

Patting my chest, she grinned at me. "Let me just fix those strands. Then we can go celebrate with dessert."

Arguing would be a waste of my time. "I'll hold the ladder."

THERE WERE SO many cars in the driveway, I had to park near the gate. Mindy hadn't let go of my hand since we'd gotten back into the truck, and she squeezed my fingers as she laughed. "Looks like we have some company."

"I invited a few people over for dessert. To celebrate." I kissed her again before reaching for the door. "Your friends are here. Our friends are here, and I even had Mad Dog bring Sir over."

"He'll be thrilled that his people will be living in the same house."

"I think so. And he'll be safer. But I think I'll build him a catio. You know, one of those enclosed spaces where he can run around outside without being eaten."

"You feed me. You love my cat. And you look incredible in a pair of Wranglers. You're perfect for me."

"We're perfect for each other. You taught me that falling in loves means finding the one who doesn't walk away when my flawed parts are bared. I'm far from perfect. You know that, but you love me anyway." I dragged my thumb across her bottom lip, appreciating what it meant that'd she'd shown me her hurts and flaws. "Thank you for trusting me with yours."

She smiled, then shook her head. "It's not a wonder I've been attracted to you since you caught me at the bottom of that ladder. Our hearts knew what our brains didn't."

"And it only took us this long to figure it out." I walked around and opened her door. "Let's go celebrate our good news. There are a lot of people happy for us. Either that or they're here for that chocolate cake you love so much."

She slipped her hand in mine. "Lead the way, cowboy."

Hopefully, she didn't want a long engagement because I couldn't wait to see her walking up the aisle. Now I knew what happily ever after was like, and it tasted good.

EPILOGUE

STEPHANIE

"Get back here, you toots!" Hollering was futile, but I did it anyway.

I couldn't believe this was happening today. Holding onto my tiara with one hand, I dialed Joji as I chased after the ornery llamas. At this rate, there was no way I was making it to meet Jeffrey and Mindy on time.

Or we'd just have two extra creatures with us when we talked about the wedding. Maybe Jeffrey knew something about herding llamas. Or Mindy. It was probably closer to herding cats than cattle.

My main goal now was to keep them away from the grapevines.

"Hello." Joji sounded chipper, which meant she didn't know her beloved spitters were loose.

"There are two llamas booking it through the winery. Any chance they're yours?"

"Well, crap. That new goat keeps scaring them off. I'm sorry. I'll head over." She sighed. "Chasing them only makes it worse. But they usually come when I call."

Clint and the llamas had that in common.

As I slowed my pace, a lasso spun in the air.

"Don't rope the llamas!" I rushed around the trees to see who was trying to lasso a llama.

Blake Dalton.

I hadn't seen him since the night he'd come to tell me that Liam had died. What was Blake doing here?

Shaking my head, I pulled down the hem of my obnoxiously pink T-shirt. "Of course you'd try to rope them. This isn't a rodeo, Blake."

Blake tipped his hat. "Hey there. Aren't you looking fancy?" He sauntered up in the way only a rodeo cowboy could and reached out. "Your halo is a bit crooked there."

"It's a tiara."

"Same difference."

I hugged him. It had been five years since the rodeo accident that took Liam's life, and his best friend hadn't called in all that time. Stepping back, I swiped at my wild curls, then propped my hands on my hips. "It's been a long time. What brings you here?"

"I'm meeting someone who needs a carpenter. He wants an arbor or something. And a new restaurant. I wondered if I'd see you today."

"A bigger restaurant. And you better not have come to this winery without making a point of finding me."

Blake and Liam had been best friends since grade school. Then they'd ridden the rodeo circuit together. Seeing Blake brought back a flood of memories, and I blinked, hoping to hold back tears.

"If I'd known I'd make you cry, I wouldn't have come." He flashed his signature half smile.

"It's good to see you." I leaned around the trees and spotted the llamas. "Know anything about herding animals that spit?"

"Nope. Marriage wasn't really my thing." He winked. "Come on. We'll figure it out. How hard can it be?"

"Oh, no. They're like cats." I stepped back. "Since they aren't running anymore, we'll watch them from here until Joji arrives."

He tilted his head and read my shirt. "Maid of Honor. Who's getting married?"

"My brother. He met someone who is perfect for him." My phone buzzed. "Speak of the devil." I swiped to answer. "Jeffrey, hi. Sorry I'm late. Got a bit distracted on the way. But I'll be there soon."

He chuckled. "No problem. I was just concerned because—"

"I know. I'm never late. But there's a first time for everything."

"Yep. I have to agree with you about that. See you in a bit." He ended the call.

Standing where I could see the llamas, I asked, "So you're the carpenter on the restaurant expansion?"

"Yes, ma'am. I figured it was time to stop by. I've been a stranger too long. Then I met a guy I did some work for once, and he asked me to do a job. I didn't know it was here at your winery until later." He stuffed his hands in his pockets. "Sorry I was gone so long. And for skipping the funeral. I just . . ."

I rubbed his arm. "You don't have to explain. I get it."

"You look good, Steph."

"Thanks. You too. Looks like you even shaved."

He glanced back as Joji jogged toward us. "First impressions and all that."

"Where are my babies?" Joji smiled as she walked up.

"That way." Blake hooked a thumb toward the escapees. "Steph wouldn't let me lasso them, so we're just babysitting from here."

Joji lifted an eyebrow as she looked at Blake. "You're new. I'm Joji."

"Blake Dalton. Nice to make your acquaintance."

"Are you a friend of Stephanie's?" She started walking toward the llamas but kept her body turned toward him.

"Something like that." He pointed behind her. "It's safer if you look in the same direction you walk."

"Yep." Joji spun around and stopped. "Simon, Garfunkel! Come here, boys."

Two white heads swung around, and those two llamas looked as if they were smiling as they trotted toward Joji.

She fed them each a piece of apple. "Sorry they bothered y'all."

Simon and Garfunkel walked alongside Joji as she headed back across the road to the goat farm.

"Now that you've met the llamas, I'll introduce you to the bride and groom." I led him down the walkway, then veered off the main path and followed the walking trail toward the creek where we'd agreed to meet.

Jeffrey and Mindy were wrapped in each other's arms, kissing like no one was watching.

"Let me guess. Those are the kids getting married." Another one of those half smiles lit up Blake's face. "They're cute. I'll give them that."

I cleared my throat. "Sorry we're late. Joji's llamas decided on an excursion."

Jeffrey's head whipped around. "Llamas?"

"Look at that shirt!" Mindy laughed and squeezed Jeffrey's arm. "You should get Mad Dog one to match."

"He'd probably prefer if it said *Best Man* rather than *Maid of Honor*, but I'm sure he'd love that color and all those shiny things. I need sunglasses just to look at you." He shook his head, then pointed beside me. "You must be Blake."

"Yep, at least I was last time I checked." He stuck out his hand. "I hear congratulations are in order."

Jeffrey smiled at Mindy. "This is my fiancée, Mindy."

"Blake Dalton."

I stepped up closer to Blake. "Jeffrey, do you remember Blake? He was at my wedding."

Jeffrey's brow furrowed. "I'm sorry. I don't."

Blake shrugged. "No worries. I didn't remember meeting you either. We were all younger then."

Responding to Jeffrey's still-furrowed brow, I explained the connection. "Blake was a friend of Liam's."

"Oh." Jeffrey let go of Mindy and motioned for me to follow him. We walked a few paces up the path before he spoke again. "I'm sorry. I didn't know."

I patted his chest, looking up at him. "I'm fine. Really. You don't need to find a different carpenter. Blake is a good guy."

Not only would Blake be building the romantic little arbor, but he'd be here at the winery every day while construction happened at the restaurant. This was the universe's way of making me deal with my grief. I'd worked through some of it, but there was a bag labeled guilt that I shoved under mounds of dirt whenever I thought about it. And now, when my brother was about to get married, burying that guilt wasn't an option. I couldn't look at Blake without thinking of Liam. The universe had crap timing.

I nudged Jeffrey back toward Mindy. "Let's go figure what needs to be done for the wedding. Blake's being here is not a problem."

"You'll tell me if it is?"

Not a chance. "Yes."

Mindy and Blake stopped talking as Jeffrey and I walked up.

Blake hitched up his jeans. "I could build it at night if

you'd rather not look at me." Humor showed up as crinkles near his brown eyes.

I'd missed his sense of humor. "We'll have to see, but I'll keep that in mind."

"You do that." He rubbed my shoulder. "And when you're done with that shirt, I might have a use for it. When I haul long pieces of lumber in the bed of the truck, I tie something bright and awful to the end. So the other drivers notice."

"Are you calling my shirt ugly?"

He shook his head. "No, ma'am. I'm calling it noticeable."

Jeffrey laughed. "That's one way of putting it." He dipped his head and whispered to Mindy loud enough the squirrels on other side of the creek could hear him. "That's not the color you chose for the wedding, is it?"

She quirked an eyebrow and grinned. "What? You don't like it?"

"I'm not telling you no because I know how that would end. We'd all need sunglasses at the wedding." He poked her in the side before giving her a quick kiss.

Blake laced his fingers together and rested them on top his head. "They always like that?"

I nodded, my tiara sliding back and forth as I did. "Even before they liked each other. But you'll get used to it."

"I doubt that." He worked his ever-present toothpick from one side of his mouth to the other. "Sappier than what I'm used to."

"Mindy and Jeffrey are like a good snack—sweet and salty." I straightened my sparkly headpiece.

"Working here might be entertaining then."

"That's one way to describe it." I shoved my hands in my pockets, acknowledging that I'd missed Blake and appreciated the reminder of Liam.

"The nice thing about working at a winery is that there's

lots of wine around," Jeffrey said with a chuckle. "And I'll make sure you don't starve."

"Blake doesn't drink wine." I remembered the time Liam had begged Blake to taste a sip after the winery had first opened.

"Hate the stuff. Grapes are okay, but all smashed up? Nah."

Mindy stepped closer to me, her smile promising humor. "At least you know he won't be sneaking bottles out of here in his pant leg or anything."

How had our conversation gotten so off course? "The wedding." I clapped my hands. "We need to focus."

Blake stood up straight and squared his shoulders. "Yes, ma'am."

Seeing Blake sparked a worry that I'd fall apart, but here I was laughing.

Maybe the universe deserved more credit for its timing.

PRAYING my waterproof mascara was truly waterproof, I waited for my cue to walk to the front. Mindy and I were tucked behind a beautifully made room divider, hidden from the guests.

I kept my breathing steady and rolled my shoulders. The ribbon wrapped around the stems of my bouquet were drenched from my sweaty palms.

Mindy leaned in close. "I invited Blake to the wedding."

"Why?"

"Because of the way you look at him." She nudged me. "Just returning the favor you did for me."

"I appreciate it, but Blake was Liam's best friend. They'd known each other since they were kids. He makes me laugh, but he's not someone I could ever date."

She motioned toward the rows of seats as Blake sat in a chair near the back. "At some point, you might want to talk to him about that." Then she pressed a hand to my back. "Your turn. And hurry because I'm more than ready to marry your brother."

Everyone here knew that.

Easing around the divider, I stole a glance at Blake before walking up the aisle. I focused on my brother, delighted by his elated expression. Behind me, Blake watched my every step. I could feel his stare.

After hugging my brother, I took my place in front. Mad Dog, Jeffrey, and I were the only ones up here because Mad Dog was acting as both the pastor and the best man. That was a combination I'd never seen before.

I let my gaze slide to Blake. I'd never seen him in a suit before. Well, almost a suit. Instead of suit pants he wore pressed Wranglers. But overall, he cleaned up rather nicely. The man had even shaved again.

When he winked, I snapped my focus to where Mindy stood at the end of the aisle, smiling like all her dreams were coming true.

I was thrilled and honored to be here for the beginning of their happily ever after.

∾

READ about Stephanie and Blake in *Captivated by Steph*.

Keep Reading for a BONUS epilogue!

BONUS EPILOGUE

JEFFREY

I strolled through the tables, visualizing how the room would look with customers at each one. All my dreams for the restaurant had come true. And my personal life was like a late-in-life fairy tale.

Lights draped among the open rafters all twinkled to life at once, and Laurel squealed. "It's magical. What time will she be here?"

Frustration bubbled up, and I sucked in a deep breath before turning to face her. "You were supposed to message Mindy."

That signature Laurel grin preceded her laugh. "Gotcha. She should be here in ten minutes, which means Mindy will be here in five." She spun her finger in a circle and headed toward the door. "I'm outta here. Holler if you need anything. Texting is easier, but—you know—whatever works best."

Alone again, I turned on the music and waited. I had a handful of my best cooks in the kitchen, making incredible food Mindy would be able to enjoy.

She'd changed all aspects of my life. Having a menu that

offered choices for those with restricted diets—whatever the reason—had increased the popularity. Waking up next to someone who lovingly challenged me was what I'd craved for a long time.

The door opened, and Mindy stepped in wearing the same gown she'd worn the first night we'd danced. "Hi."

"Happy Anniversary." I pulled her close and dipped my head to meet her lips. "I wanted a private celebration with you before tomorrow night's grand reopening."

"It's absolutely beautiful. I'm so proud of you."

"Life may get a little crazy starting tomorrow." I remembered how it had been when I first opened. Something new attracted people in droves.

Her gaze dropped as she pinched her lips, and she nodded. "It'll be good."

"We'll have to have breakfast together on the days I'll be out really late." I trailed my fingers down her back. "But you need to tell me if it's too much. The last time I went through something like this, it was just me. But now it's us."

She brushed her fingers on my cheek. "I'll tell you or at least write you a letter."

We now had an array of beautiful stationery—and a few cowboy-themed options—for us to use to write letters when we felt the need.

"Dinner will be out in a few minutes, but we have time for a dance if you'd like."

"I'd love to dance." She rested a hand on my shoulder and leaned in close. "I'm really happy, Jeffrey."

"Good. I know this past year has had its ups and down. The expansion kept us super busy, but I wouldn't trade a minute of it. I enjoyed last year more than the last ten years before it . . . combined."

"It's been amazing."

Music wafted around us, and we snuggled upright. With

her body pressed to mine, I forgot about dinner, or customers, or time in general. As the third song ended, Eric, my best chef, cleared his throat.

"I think dinner is ready." I patted Mindy's hip as I pulled out her chair.

Two beautifully plated appetizers appeared in front of us. "Our first course is grilled shrimp with peaches."

Mindy smiled and stared at her plate. After taking a bite, her face went pale, and she jumped out of her chair. With a hand slapped over her mouth, she raced toward the ladies' room.

Eric grabbed the back of a chair. "I swear I followed your recipe exactly, and I made sure nothing else was being prepped in that kitchen. Mr. Carpenter, I promise you."

"Okay. Let me check on her. Maybe I messed up on something." I dragged my fingers through my hair as I stepped into the bathroom. "Sweetheart, I'm so sorry."

"I'm okay." She stood and fanned her face.

I wet a paper towel and dabbed her cheeks. "I thought I knew everything that would trigger problems. Later, when you feel better, you can tell me where I messed up."

She shook her head. "You didn't mess up."

I cradled her face, then kissed her forehead. "I can have them clear that off the table. Then we'll try the next course."

Her fingers tangled with mine. "No need. I should be okay. Let's go back out there."

I let her lead me through the room. Tonight was supposed to be perfect for her. I wanted her to enjoy a five-course meal without a single worry. What had I done wrong?

She sat down and reached for her purse. As I took the chair next to her, she handed me a letter. "You didn't mess up, Jeffrey. You succeeded. At least I hope you see it that way."

That cleared things up completely. Not.

Hoping the letter offered more information, I tore it open, then slipped my readers out of my pocket. I hated that these were necessary for the words to be clear on the page.

Dear Jeffrey,

You're going to be a daddy.

I'm not sure Sir Lancelot will be happy about the news, but I hope you are.

Mindy

I blinked several times before braving a look at her. Men my age were grandpas, not brand-new dads. New dads didn't need readers to read the announcement.

"Are you upset?" She squeezed my hand.

A head shake would have to suffice until I recovered my voice. "Shocked. I'm . . . I mean you're . . . I'm not calling you old or anything, but I didn't expect this."

Her eyes filled with tears. "I didn't either, but . . ." Her shoulders bounced, and I wasn't sure if she were shrugging or if sobs were coming.

I touched her cheek. "But underneath the shock, I'm excited. Truly."

"What if . . ." She wiped her eyes and choked back a sob.

"You'll be a wonderful mom. Absolutely. Sir Lancelot can attest to that."

Her lips twitched into a small smile even as tears slipped down her cheeks. "You aren't upset?"

"Not in the least." A to-do list started in my head. "There's so much to do. I need to childproof the house. We'll have to fence in the pool or maybe get rid of it altogether. And I'll have Mad Dog find a horse that's good with kids."

Laughter bubbled out of Mindy, and she popped a shrimp in her mouth. Tears still glistened in her eyes, but shock did that to people.

"It's a tiny bit early to be buying our kid a horse. We have time for childproofing and putting up fencing. I'm glad you aren't disappointed." She pointed at her plate. "This is the best thing I've ever tasted."

I stared at this beautiful woman, the mother of my child. "It wasn't the food at all."

"I started feeling yuck a few days ago, and now, every time I see food, I get sick. Then I'm fine for a few hours. I meant to make myself a plate before getting dressed, but I forgot because I was so nervous." She ran a hand over her stomach. "If I were any farther along, I wouldn't have fit in this dress." Tears flowed in earnest now. "I gave up my dreams of being a mom a long time ago. It didn't seem possible. So thank you." She hugged my neck. "I love you, Mr. Carpenter."

I leaned in to kiss her, and she shook her head. I pressed a kiss to her forehead instead. "I love you too. And I'm looking forward to the adventure that will be our life. It won't be perfect, but it'll be ours."

～

If you loved this story, please consider leaving a review.

And to read about Tessa and Garrett, grab *Two Risks I'd Never Take Again*. It's book 6 in the Never Say Never series.

A NOTE TO READERS

Thank you for reading!

Jeffrey first appeared in *Enchanted by Joji,* and readers asked if he was going to get a story. Now he has one!

The snowstorm and power outage were inspired by the storm in Texas lest year. I lost power for days, and it snowed in San Antonio twice during the week. As I'm uploading this book, we are about to be under another winter storm watch, which is crazy for Texas.

Be sure to check out my website for updates about the series and for information about my other books.

www.RemiCarrington.com

ABOUT THE AUTHOR

Remi Carrington is a figment of Pamela Humphrey's imagination. She loves romance & chocolate, enjoys disappearing into a delicious book, and considers people-watching a sport. She was born in the pages of the novel *Just You* and then grew into an alter ego.

She writes sweet romance and romantic comedies set in Texas. Her books are part of the Phrey Press imprint.

facebook.com/remiromance
twitter.com/phreypress
instagram.com/phreypress

Printed in Great Britain
by Amazon

30417668R00153